Will I get osteoporosis?

How do I know if my bone density is low?

What is a DXA test?

How do I interpret my results?

What kinds of nutrients and exercise can help improve my bone density?

The Bone Density Test can help you find the answers to these questions and more—with clear information and straightforward advice that tells women what they need to know for a longer, stronger, healthier life.

THE
BONE DENSITY TEST

Other Books by the Author

THE CELLULITE BREAKTHROUGH
HAIR SAVERS FOR WOMEN: A COMPLETE GUIDE TO
PREVENTING AND TREATING HAIR LOSS
NATURAL WEIGHT LOSS MIRACLES
21 DAYS TO BETTER FITNESS
KAVA: THE ULTIMATE GUIDE TO NATURE'S ANTI-STRESS HERB

Other Books Coauthored by the Author

LEAN BODIES
LEAN BODIES TOTAL FITNESS
30 DAYS TO SWIMSUIT LEAN
HIGH PERFORMANCE NUTRITION
POWER EATING
SHAPE TRAINING
HIGH PERFORMANCE BODYBUILDING
50 WORKOUT SECRETS
BUILT! THE NEW BODYBUILDING FOR EVERYONE

Most Berkley Books are available at special quantity discounts for bulk purchases for sales promotions, premiums, fund-raising, or educational use. Special books, or book excerpts, can also be created to fit specific needs.

For details, write: Special Markets, The Berkley Publishing Group, 375 Hudson Street, New York, New York 10014.

The
Bone
Density
Test

Maggie Greenwood-Robinson, Ph.D.

BERKLEY BOOKS, NEW YORK

To my dear friend Debbra Dunning Skidmore

NOTE: Every effort has been made to ensure that the information contained in this book is complete and accurate. However, neither the publisher nor the author is engaged in rendering professional advice or services to the individual reader. The ideas, procedures, and suggestions contained in this book are not intended as a substitute for consulting with your physician. All matters regarding your health require medical supervision. Neither the author nor the publisher shall be liable or responsible for any loss, injury, or damage allegedly arising from any information or suggestion in this book.

THE BONE DENSITY TEST

A Berkley Book / published by arrangement with
the author

PRINTING HISTORY
Berkley edition / October 2000

All rights reserved.
Copyright © 2000 by Maggie Greenwood-Robinson.
Book design by Tiffany Kukec.
Cover design by Erika Fusari.
This book, or parts thereof, may not be
reproduced in any form without permission.
For information address: The Berkley Publishing Group, a
division of Penguin Putnam Inc., 375 Hudson Street,
New York, New York 10014.

The Penguin Putnam Inc. World Wide Web site address is
http://www.penguinputnam.com

ISBN: 0-425-17782-3

BERKLEY®
Berkley Books are published by The Berkley Publishing Group,
a division of Penguin Putnam Inc., 375 Hudson Street,
New York, New York 10014.
BERKLEY and the "B" design
are trademarks belonging to Penguin Putnam Inc.

PRINTED IN THE UNITED STATES OF AMERICA

10 9 8 7 6 5 4 3 2 1

Contents

Acknowledgments

I gratefully thank the following people for their work and contributions to this book: Anthony Perkins, M.D., chairman of the Radiology Department at Methodist Hospital in Henderson, Kentucky, for reviewing pertinent parts of the manuscript relating to bone density testing and technology; the women who willingly shared their experiences with bone density testing; my agent, Madeleine Morel, 2M Communications, Ltd.; Christine Zika and the staff at The Berkley Publishing Group; and my husband, Jeff, for love and patience during the research and writing of this book.

Introduction

The Test That Can Save Your Life

L ike most women, you know it's vital to have a mammogram and a Pap test on regular occasions. Both tests can help save your life by discovering breast and cervical cancers in their earliest stages, when they are the most curable.

In addition, you probably have your cholesterol tested and your blood pressure checked at regular intervals. Both can save your life too—by monitoring for signs of heart disease. Heart disease is the leading killer of American women today. It claims more lives than all forms of cancer combined, even breast cancer.

But did you know there's another life-saving test you should have, particularly as you approach, enter, and pass through midlife?

The test you should have is a bone density test, also known as a bone densitometry test.

It's a test that can help save you from infirmity and disability later in life. It's a test that can help stretch out your productive years and quality of life. And it's a test that improves the early detection and treatment of osteoporosis—a bone-thinning disease that can cause crippling fractures and that results in as many deaths a year as breast cancer. It's a test that can save your life.

How Does a Bone Density Test Work?

Many different kinds of bone density tests are used to screen for, diagnose, and manage osteoporosis. All bone density tests, however, ascertain the amount of bone in specific areas of your skeleton and evaluate their *density*. Density refers to the quantity of mineral (predominantly calcium) found in any given area or volume of bone. The strength of your bones depends on how dense they are.

The bones most commonly measured are those in the lower spine and hip regions. These sites are assessed because most osteoporotic fractures occur there. Sometimes, a doctor may recommend a whole body test, particularly if you have a disease or take a medication that causes bones to degenerate.

A bone density test is the most accurate method for assessing bone health. For predicting the risk of fracture, it is more accurate than measuring blood pressure to predict strokes; cholesterol to predict heart attacks; or mammograms to find breast cancer.

Writing in a 1999 issue of the *International Journal of Fertility and Women's Medicine,* physicians Carolina Kulak and John P. Bilezikian noted: "One looks forward to the day when bone mass measurement will be as much a standard for preventive care as is measurement of blood pressure, blood sugar, blood cholesterol, or mammography."

Why Is the Test Performed?

Bone mineral density testing can:

- Confirm a diagnosis of osteoporosis.

- Determine your risk for fracture.

- Track your rate of bone loss, or bone gain, by repeating the test at regular intervals.

- Provide information that helps your physician identify treatments to protect your bone health. These treatments may include hormone replacement therapy (HRT) and other medications.

- Help you decide whether to choose hormone replacement therapy (HRT).

- Monitor whether a particular treatment is slowing or stopping bone loss.

- Establish a baseline measurement for bone density against which future test results can be compared.

Your physician may recommend that you have a bone density test for other reasons too—for example, if you suffer from certain diseases or take medications known to deplete bone.

Who Should Get a Bone Density Test?

Bone loss starts at around age 30 or 35 and is progressive—which is why it is so vital to diagnose it early with a bone density test. At present, there is lots of debate among osteoporosis experts as to which patients should have bone density tests, and various medical organizations have established their own guidelines on this issue. Below is an overview of testing recommendations made by various organizations.

The National Osteoporosis Foundation recommends testing if:

- You are over 65 years old.

- You are postmenopausal with more than one risk factor. (For information on risk factors, see chapter 2.)

- You are postmenopausal with a fracture.

- You are considering treatment for osteoporosis.

- You have been on hormone replacement therapy (HRT) for a prolonged period of time.

The Foundation for Osteoporosis Research and Education (FORE) recommends testing if:

- You are perimenopausal or postmenopausal and are not taking hormone replacement therapy (HRT), refuse HRT, would use test results to make decisions about HRT, or would take HRT for the prevention or treatment of osteoporosis.

- You are at risk for osteoporosis, five years past menopause, and have never had a bone density test.

- You want to stop taking HRT in favor of an alternative treatment.

- You are taking HRT, but have other risk factors, or a new fracture.

- You have had an X ray that suspects or detects osteoporosis.

- You are taking steroid medications or other bone-weakening drugs.

- You have mild primary hyperparathyroidism (an overproduction of parathyroid hormone—a disease that causes bone loss).

- You are premenopausal, over age 30, and have multiple risk factors for osteoporosis.

- You are over age 65 and have not had a previous bone density test.

- You have a nonviolent fracture (occurring from a force equal to or less than a fall from standing height).

- You're on drug therapy to treat osteoporosis (as a way of monitoring treatment).

- You have bone loss that is being monitored.

The American Association of Clinical Endocrinologists (AACE) recommends testing if:

- You are perimenopausal or postmenopausal, concerned about osteoporosis, and open to treatment—as a way to assess your risk.

- You have had X rays that suggest the presence of osteoporosis.

- You are beginning or receiving long-term corticosteroid treatment.

- You are perimenopausal or postmenopausal with hyperparathyroidism.

- You are undergoing treatment for osteoporosis, as a tool to monitor the effectiveness of therapy.

In addition to the above guidelines, many bone specialists recommend testing for women who have no specific risk factors for osteoporosis, but are concerned that they may develop it.

Writing in *Clinical Therapeutics,* Pierre J. Meunier, M.D., et al., noted: "The absence of risk factors does not mean that a woman's bone mineral density is normal or that a fracture will not occur. Therefore, if available, bone mineral density testing should be offered to these patients."

If any of the recommendations described above fit your situation, talk to your doctor about getting a bone mineral density test.

What You Don't Know Could Hurt You

What's frightening is the lack of awareness among women about bone density tests—and about the treatment of osteoporosis in general. One survey of one thousand women discovered that 60 percent were unaware that a medical test could diagnose osteoporosis, according to the National Osteoporosis Foundation.

In addition, a survey conducted by *Prevention/NBC Today* found that only one in four women over the age of 50 said their physicians had recommended a bone density test—a test that can save lives!

Here are some other startling statistics, based on a Gallup Poll survey of American women, aged 45 to 75:

- Three out of every four women have never discussed osteoporosis with their physicians (which implies they haven't talked about bone density tests, either), even though osteoporosis may strike one in every two women.

- Seven out of ten women considered at high risk for osteoporosis have never discussed the disease with their physician. Nearly 70 percent of these women say they don't see a need to discuss it or aren't concerned about the disease.

- One in four women who say they are familiar with the disease believe there is no treatment or prevention for osteoporosis. Please note: Numerous treatments are available to prevent bone loss and reduce your odds of fracture. Having a bone density test can give you vital information to help decide on a course of treatment. What's more, the test can monitor the effects of diet, exercise, and treatments on your bone status.

Fortunately, you can now benefit from scientific advances in diagnostic technology and in treatment options. Bone densitometry tests used to be available mostly at major medical centers and therefore were not readily accessible to women living in small towns and rural areas. But not anymore. Bone densitometry equipment has moved from the medical center to doctors' offices and is available in mobile units and nonmedical locations.

Take advantage of this technology, or else a diagnosis of osteoporosis could come too late—when you suffer a crippling fracture. A fracture indicates that a lot of bone has been lost and your bones are in pretty bad shape.

When osteoporosis is diagnosed early with the help of a bone density test, preventive therapies can be prescribed to help prevent fractures. The sooner bone loss is detected, the sooner you can start doing something about it. With a bone density test, you can fight osteoporosis and keep it from robbing your independence, health, and vitality.

One of the many positive effects of having a bone density test is that the results may alter your behavior and your lifestyle—for the better.

Let's meet several women who are doing just that.

Women Who Took the Test

When Nina L., aged 49, asked if she should have her bone density tested, her family doctor replied, "No reason to."

Still, she wanted one—basically as a yardstick against which potential future bone loss could be measured in subsequent tests. Her only risk factors were that she is Caucasian and had been a smoker for about thirteen years, from age 20 to age 33. So Nina appealed to her gynecologist, who agreed to order the test.

The results of Nina's bone density test were favorable, showing healthy bone mass in her spine and hip.

Nina attributes the favorable report to a combination of factors. Since her midthirties, she has regularly engaged in weight-bearing exercises, primarily aerobics. She has also played racquetball regularly. Exercise stimulates the formation of bone.

In the past several years, Nina has added weight training to her routine. Today, she trains with weights three times a week for thirty minutes each session. In addition, she regularly walks for additional exercise, as well as to fight some arthritis she has in her spine. Part of her walking routine involves pushing her twenty-five-pound granddaughter in a stroller around the neighborhood. "I actually feel stronger now than I ever have," she says.

Although not a milk drinker, Nina has always eaten a healthy diet. For the last twelve years, she has taken vitamin-mineral supplements, along with calcium supplements. Her calcium intake is roughly 1,200 milligrams a day, exactly what her body needs at this stage in life for good bone health.

More recently, Nina's gynecologist prescribed hormone replacement therapy (HRT) because tests revealed low hormone levels. HRT is frequently recommended to prevent and reverse bone loss. The decision to go on HRT was not made without serious deliberation, however.

"I weighed the good and the bad of HRT," Nina explained. "My doctor told me I could die of heart disease or complications of a broken hip before I would die of breast cancer. She feels that women should go on HRT for a few years so that they don't lose bone during menopause and to protect the heart."

Since undergoing HRT, Nina has had no adverse side effects and feels that this therapy is one more anti-osteoporosis measure she can take to counteract the rapid bone loss that typically occurs during menopause.

(For more information about HRT and other drugs used to treat osteoporosis, see chapter 10.)

In 1997, Mary Jane A. had her yearly routine physical examination. After taking a height measurement, the nurse noticed that Mary Jane had shrunk about three inches. Loss of height can signal loss of bone. Concerned, Mary Jane's doctor ordered a bone density test.

(Mary Jane remeasured herself at home and found that she had lost only a quarter of an inch from her normal five foot, five inch frame.)

The first test scanned her hip region only. It revealed that she was moderately "osteopenic"—meaning that there was some loss of bone, but that she did not yet have full-blown osteoporosis.

At the time, Mary Jane was 61 years old. Based on the results, her physician recommended that she increase her calcium intake from 500 milligrams a day to 1,000 milligrams a day and take a calcium supplement formulated with vitamin D. He also suggested that she begin a regular program of weight-bearing exercise.

Since then, Mary Jane has been working out three times a week. Each exercise session includes thirty minutes of treadmill walking followed by thirty minutes of exercise on Nautilus weight-training machines.

In addition to these lifestyle adjustments, her physician prescribed a regimen of 0.5 milligrams of Fosamax a day. Fosamax is a nonhormonal drug approved by the U.S. Food and Drug Administration (FDA) for the prevention of fractures and for the treatment of osteoporosis.

HRT was not an option for Mary Jane because of a history of breast cancer in her family. Both her mother and grandmother died from the disease. What's more, Mary Jane has in the past suffered from phlebitis and has varicosities. These medical conditions make HRT unadvisable.

To evaluate whether Fosamax was doing its job, her physician ordered a follow-up bone density test a year later. There was good news: The bone density in her hip had increased. The second test also measured bone density in her spine. Her score for the spine showed mild osteopenia, the earliest stage of bone loss.

Initially, Mary Jane had no adverse side effects from taking Fosamax. She later experienced some gastrointestinal irritation. Upon the advice of her physician, she discontinued the drug for three weeks. Mary Jane has resumed Fosamax therapy and plans to continue the medication as part of a total anti-osteoporosis program.

Low back pain that began approximately 12 years ago sent June D. to an orthopedic specialist for relief. A conventional X ray revealed low bone mass in her spine. At the time, a full back cast was advised—a recommendation that was untenable because June is a librarian. "I have to bend, stoop, and be mobile while working. I couldn't be in a cast."

Some additional tests uncovered a hormone imbalance. A low dose of estrogen in combination with progestin was prescribed; however, June would go off and on the prescription. "But every time I stopped taking the pills, the back pain would return."

In 1992, June had a complete hysterectomy because she was suffering from heavy bleeding and fibroids, an overgrowth of muscle tissue that makes up the wall of the uterus. After the procedure, she began a permanent regimen of estrogen.

A hysterectomy is a risk factor for osteoporosis. In addition, June had several other risk factors for the disease, including being female, Caucasian, and postmenopausal, as well as having a prior smoking history. She is also lactose intolerant, which means she cannot properly digest milk. Her height loss over the years has totaled approximately three inches.

In 1999, June had her initial bone density test. It diagnosed full-fledged osteoporosis. In the test report, the radiologist noted that compared to the norm, June had 72 percent of normal bone density in her lumbar spine (lower back); 77 percent of normal bone density in her hip; and 87 percent of normal bone density in her wrist.

The report also explained that June's risk for fracture was increased six times for her spine, three and a half times for her hip, and three times for her wrist—predictions based on her bone density measurements.

Her doctor prescribed Fosamax, but June suffered side effects, including severe upper gastrointestinal pain and heartburn. She had to be treated temporarily with a heartburn drug.

In addition to taking estrogen, June takes 1,000 milligrams a day of Viactiv, a supplement that contains calcium, vitamin D, and vitamin K. She also drinks calcium-fortified juice and eats salmon with bones, a food that is rich in calcium. Although her gastrointestinal problems interfered with her ability to exercise, June plans to resume an exercise program. From now on, she will have an annual bone density test to monitor the health of her bones.

Osteoporosis can run in families—which is why June's daughter, Debbie S., has been concerned about getting the disease.

"I have always had rounded shoulders, a condition that seems to be getting worse over the years," she says. "I had fears of someday having the hunched, rounded back (called "dowager's hump") that can be a sign of low bone mass. With my mom's history, I also thought I probably had the beginnings of osteoporosis too."

Debbie, aged 49, has other risk factors besides heredity. She is Caucasian, has small bones, and used to smoke.

Certain she had some bone loss, Debbie had her first bone density test in April 2000. Imagine her surprise when the test revealed normal bone density in her hip and spine!

These results echo what many bone specialists emphasize: The presence of risk factors does not always mean a sentence of osteoporosis. Further, Debbie's case illustrates that preventive measures, initiated early, can change your genetic fate. For example, Debbie has been taking birth control pills formulated with a low dose of estrogen. Estrogen protects against bone loss.

She also takes calcium supplements in the form of Tums, an antacid that contains calcium. To ensure an additional supply of calcium, Debbie regularly drinks calcium-fortified juice and eats salmon, a fish that is high in calcium.

Her next step is to resume a regular exercise program. Not fond of exercising, the public relations consultant has been unable to find an activity that holds her interest. And it isn't for lack of trying.

"For several years, low-impact aerobics classes worked for me, until I got so tired of them I could hardly make myself go," she said. "But knowing that an active lifestyle is a protective factor for osteoporosis, I'm more motivated than ever to attend aerobics classes now."

For eight years, Delois G. watched her mother's health rapidly deteriorate, partially due to severe osteoporosis. "I was shocked by how disabling this disease is. In fact, it frightened me into having a bone density test," she said.

Delois, aged 46, underwent a full body scan. Results revealed bone loss in her lower spine and hip, but not in her forearms. Even though Delois was aware that genetics are a risk factor for osteoporosis, she was startled by the results, considering her young age. However, she also learned that she is entering menopause—a period of life when bone loss can accelerate.

Delois immediately started taking 1,500 milligrams of calcium daily, but found that supplementation caused constipation. Rather than supplement, she upped her intake of calcium-packed foods, including milk and yogurt.

Delois commutes daily from her home in New Jersey to New York City and, like many working women, finds it difficult to fit exercise into a twelve-hour workday. Her solution: fast walking in the morning from the train station to her office, and back to the station after work, for a total of thirty minutes of exercise, five days a week. Walking is a bone-conserving exercise.

Take the Test

If you're an average American woman, you have a fifty-fifty chance of getting osteoporosis. It could happen after menopause—when bone loss speeds up—or it could strike much earlier. Chronic pain, disfigurement, fractured hips, or even death could be your fate.

But it doesn't have to be. A bone density test is a fortune teller of sorts. It can forewarn you whether osteoporosis is in your cards in time to save your bones—and your life.

Isn't it time you took the test?

1.
What's Happening to My Bones?

If you could take a microscopic tour of your bones, you'd be astounded by the sights. Bone is complex, living tissue, permeated with blood vessels, nerves, and specialized cells.

There are two types of bone tissue: *cortical* bone and *trabecular* bone. Cortical bone is very dense, while trabecular bone is spongy and porous.

Cortical bone tissue envelops the hard outer surface of bone and makes up about 80 percent of the skeleton. Pinkish white in color, it is contoured to hold the numerous insertions of ligaments and muscles. Cortical bone is covered with a specialized form of connective tissue called the *periosteum*. It contains bone-forming cells called *osteoblasts*. With age, this layer becomes thinner, but never really disappears.

Underneath the cortical bone is trabecular bone tissue, a fine weave of small bony filaments that resembles foam. Because of its spongy composition, trabecular bone acts as a shock absorber when stress is applied to bones. Trabecular bone, however, is very vulnerable to osteoporosis. At the core of the bone is the soft, deep-red marrow, which manufactures blood cells.

All bones have cortical and trabecular tissue; however, they vary in the amount of each. The bones of your arms and legs, for example, are made mostly of cortical bone, with some trabecular bone at either end. By contrast, the vertebrae of your spine are mostly trabecular bone encased by a thin cortical shell.

Bone Protein: The Reinforcers

Structurally, both cortical and trabecular bones are made of a lattice of tough protein fibers, otherwise known as the bone matrix. The protein fibers include *collagen, glycoproteins*, and *proteoglycans.*

Collagen is the most abundant protein in the body and one of its strongest tissues. It helps reinforce bone and make it strong.

Although distributed mostly in the bones, cartilage, ligaments, and tendons (collectively known as connective tissue), collagen also gives shape to vital organs. It forms a fine scaffolding for organ cells and blood vessels so that they can arrange themselves into their characteristic shapes. Collagen literally binds our bodies together.

A glycoprotein is a single protein molecule linked to one carbohydrate molecule. Along with collagen, glycoproteins help reinforce bones to keep them from being too brittle.

Proteoglycans are similar to glycoproteins, but consist of a single protein molecule linked to chains of carbohydrate. Proteoglycans have the consistency of half-set

Jell-O. Their job is similar to that of collagen and gly-coproteins: to reinforce connective tissue, including bones. Proteoglycans also help activate certain cells involved in bone metabolism.

Calcium and Other Bone-Strengthening Minerals

Embedded in the protein fibers of bone are needle-like crystals of calcium, phosphorus, and other strengthening minerals. Calcium is the chief mineral in bone. It provides the structural strength that lets the bones support your weight and anchor your muscles. Calcium not immediately used by the body is stored in trabecular bone.

The crystals also contain phosphorus, resulting in a compound called calcium phosphate. The term *bone mineral* refers essentially to calcium phosphate. It is this compound that gives bone its strength. In fact, nearly 50 percent of bone weight is made up of calcium phosphate.

To a lesser degree, other minerals are constituents of this crystalline structure. They include magnesium, fluoride, copper, zinc, manganese, silicon, and boron. On average, two-thirds of the solid portion of bone is composed of minerals; the remaining one-third is the bone matrix. The ongoing deposit of minerals onto the protein fibers is called *mineralization*.

The combination of the strong bone matrix and its mineral crystals is like reinforced concrete, with the protein fibers resembling steel rods and the minerals as the concrete. This physiological engineering makes bone very strong, yet very flexible.

Bone Remodeling and Resorption

Throughout your life, bone regenerates itself in a repair and replacement process called *remodeling*. Remodeling helps maintain a constant level of calcium in the blood, which is vital for a healthy heart, proper blood circulation, and normal blood clotting.

During remodeling, the old bone matrix is swapped with new protein. And, like a savings account, the minerals are deposited and withdrawn—a process that takes place day in and day out.

The remodeling process is governed by two types of specialized bone cells: *osteoclasts* and *osteoblasts*. Osteoclasts are cells that break down and remove old bone tissue. They do this by secreting enzymes that dismantle the protein and mineral in bone. Tiny pits are actually dug in the bone, releasing calcium and other minerals into the bloodstream so that they can be recirculated throughout the body. In a type of recycling operation, most of the minerals lost from the bone will return and be used again to build new bone. The breakdown of bone by osteoclasts is technically known as *resorption*.

Osteoblasts build bone—in two ways. First, they fill in the pits with collagen, along with glycoproteins and proteoglycans. Then, the osteoblasts lay down more crystals of mineral. During this mineralization process, osteoblasts also produce a noncollagen protein called *osteocalcin*, an important material involved in bone hardening. The number of osteoblasts decreases with age.

Bones and Hormones

Osteoclasts and osteoblasts also regulate the body's supply of calcium—a process that is under hormonal control. After you eat foods containing calcium, the calcium is absorbed in the intestine and taken up by the bloodstream to be carried to various tissues, including bone, for use by the body. When calcium concentrations in the blood dip below a certain level, the parathyroid glands (four in number), located at the base of the neck, secrete *parathyroid hormone*. This hormone signals the osteoclasts to break down bone to keep blood calcium in the normal range.

Parathyroid hormone also tells the kidneys to convert an inactive form of vitamin D, called *calcidiol,* into an active form, *calcitriol.* Calcitriol enhances calcium absorption from the small intestine and reduces the excretion of phosphorus in the urine. Both actions counter the loss of minerals and increase their concentration in the blood.

When levels of calcium in the blood get too high, the thyroid gland secretes a hormone called *calcitonin.* It decreases osteoclast activity and increases osteoblast activity. As a result, the action of parathyroid hormone is blocked, preventing the release of calcium from bone. Calcium is then deposited back into the bones. Thus, calcium comes and goes as needed.

Another hormone—estrogen—is involved too. Estrogen is the collective name for a trio of female hormones: estradiol, secreted from the ovaries during your reproductive years; estriol, produced by the placenta during pregnancy; and estrone, secreted by the ovaries and adrenal glands and found in women after menopause. These naturally occurring estrogens are responsible for developing the female sex characteristics, regulating menstrual cycles, and maintaining normal cholesterol levels.

Estrogen retards the breakdown of bone—in two major ways. It foils parathyroid hormone's activation of osteoclasts and it stimulates the thyroid gland to secrete calcitonin. The net effect is to help regulate the deposit of calcium into your bones.

Year after year, anywhere from 10 to 30 percent of your skeleton is remodeled through the hormone-controlled action of osteoclasts and osteoblasts.

How Does Osteoporosis Affect Bones?

During the remodeling process, if minerals are withdrawn faster than they are replaced, your bones become more fragile and less dense. You may lose *bone mineral density,* which refers to the amount of calcium phosphate in your skeleton. Your bone mass peaks by about age 30. Afterward, bone breakdown overtakes bone formation, and you can lose bone density.

Over time, the loss of bone density can lead to a condition called *osteopenia,* or bone thinning. Osteopenia can develop into *osteoporosis,* a reduction in bone mineral that leads to crippling fractures, and sometimes death. The term osteoporosis comes from the Greek words *osteon,* bone, and *porus,* pore. The disease makes your bones more porous.

Although it is normal to lose some bone gradually as you age, osteoporosis involves a large amount of bone loss that endangers your health. Osteoporosis strikes mainly postmenopausal women, although it can begin its course of destruction much earlier in life.

Osteoporosis is usually referred to as a single disease. However, it is classified medically into two broad types: *primary osteoporosis* and *secondary osteoporosis.* Primary osteoporosis is further categorized into either Type I (postmenopausal or high-turnover) or Type II (age-related, "senile osteoporosis," or low-turnover).

Type I osteoporosis is characterized by an accelerated loss of bone mass that occurs when estrogen levels fall after menopause. In Type I, there can be a significant loss of trabecular bone, resulting in a higher incidence of spinal fractures. Type I osteoporosis strikes women 55 to 60 years of age or older.

Type II osteoporosis is the near-certain loss of bone mass that occurs in both men and women as a natural part of the aging process. Hip fractures are a common—and devastating—side effect of Type II osteoporosis. In Type II, you lose both cortical and trabecular bone mass. This disease afflicts people later in life, at approximately 70 years of age or older. Older women can suffer from both Type I and Type II osteoporosis.

Secondary osteoporosis may develop at any age and is a troubling side effect of certain diseases and the use of certain medications.

How Serious Is Osteoporosis?

Osteoporosis is the most common human bone disease, with 25 million sufferers in the United States alone. In women, bone loss can start as early as ages 30 to 35 at the rate of 0.5 to 1 percent a year. In the first three to five years following menopause, this can accelerate to 3 to 7 percent a year, making it possible to lose 9 to 35 percent of bone mass. By age 70, some women may lose up to 70 percent of their bone mass. The incidence of osteoporosis is expected to double by the year 2020 as more of our population ages.

Osteoporosis is responsible for 300,000 hip fractures a year. Of those who suffer osteoporosis-related hip fractures, 20 percent die within a year, and half of those who survive are never able to walk independently again. Osteoporosis is a painful, crippling disease—one that compromises independence and quality of life.

What many people don't realize is that osteoporosis is linked to 50,000 deaths annually, largely from complications of surgery or immobilization after hip fractures. In fact, you are two to four times more likely to die during the first six to twelve months after a hip fracture, particularly if you suffer from poor health already.

Even more alarming: Annually, almost as many women die from complications due to osteoporosis-related hip fractures as die of breast cancer. In fact, your risk of developing such a fracture is higher than your 9 percent risk of getting breast cancer. What's more, the lifetime risk of dying from a hip fracture is 2.8 percent for Caucasian women—the same lifetime risk you have of dying from breast cancer.

Clearly, the treatment and prevention of osteoporosis is of paramount concern. A bone density test is an excellent tool in the fight against osteoporosis.

2.

Will I Get Osteoporosis?

You might think seriously about getting a bone density test once you learn more about risk factors for osteoporosis. Risk factors are genetic, health, and lifestyle considerations that increase the likelihood that you might develop a particular disease or condition.

The risk factors discussed below are all red flags for osteoporosis, signaling that you might really need a bone density test. If so, have your doctor schedule one for the sake of your lifelong health and mobility.

A point worth mentioning here, however, is that being at risk does not mean you have osteoporosis, or that you will develop it. It simply means that you may want to take better care of your bone health, and this may include having a bone density test.

YOU'RE A WOMAN

While both sexes lose bone with age, women are at a higher risk for osteoporosis than men are. In fact, 80 percent of those afflicted with osteoporosis are women. Women's bones are smaller than men's, and naturally have less bone tissue. That means there's less of a calcium reserve when the body needs it. Further, women lose bone more rapidly than men do because of accelerated bone loss at menopause.

YOU'RE CAUCASIAN OR ASIAN

For reasons not fully known, osteoporosis is more prevalent in Caucasian and Asian women than in women of other races. At age 50, a Caucasian woman has a 54 percent chance of an osteoporotic fracture during her remaining lifetime; a 34 percent chance of spinal fracture; a 17 percent chance of hip fracture; and a 16 percent chance of wrist fracture.

Asian women may have a higher risk because of a genetic predisposition to low bone density, or possibly because of a lower supply of calcium in their diets.

Also, people of northern European descent tend to have lower bone density than people of southern European descent—although medical experts have few clues yet as to why.

Black women, on the other hand, have larger bones and higher bone density than Caucasian or Asian women. As a result, black women have roughly half the rate of hip fractures that white women have. However, as our population ages—including the black population— there will be a rise in osteoporosis among black women, according to medical investigators.

When you have a bone density test, measurements are matched to your racial or ethnic group in order to arrive at an accurate diagnosis. So if you're a white female, your test is compared and evaluated according to tests made on a group of white American women just like you.

YOU HAVE A FAMILY HISTORY OF OSTEOPOROSIS

The chances of osteoporosis catching up with you in the future has to do with your genes—the basic units of heredity that carry instructions for individual characteristics. In other words, you inherit bone density and bone strength from your parents. In fact, about 70 percent of osteoporosis cases may be attributed to hereditary influences.

Scientific studies of twins and family members have discovered that genetic makeup influences the amount of bone you build during your lifetime, as well as how fast you lose bone later in life. However, it's not yet clear exactly how much of a factor genetics play in bone loss, compared to other factors. Even so, you're probably at a higher risk if your mother or other close relative had osteoporosis.

But if osteoporosis runs in your family, take heart. Medical studies of mothers and daughters reveal that women who engage in lifelong programs of weight-bearing exercise, eat a calcium-rich diet, and/or take estrogen replacement in postmenopausal years can preserve or even increase their genetically determined bone mass. Thus, you're not doomed to the disease, as long as you adopt a bone-healthy lifestyle now.

YOU'RE UNDERGOING MENOPAUSE

Menopause is a natural stage in life that marks the end of your reproductive years. Immediately after menopause, trabecular bone is lost at a high rate. Fortunately, a good deal of this can be reversed with the appropriate treatment and healthy lifestyle habits.

There are three types of menopause: normal menopause, early menopause, and premature menopause. Bone mineral density is affected differently in each one.

Normal menopause comes naturally to women between the ages of 45 and 55, while early menopause occurs prior to age 45. Premature menopause refers to the bodily changes that take place following the surgical removal of a woman's ovaries.

During all three types of menopause, the supply of estrogen shuts down, and estrogen stays very low for the rest of your life. This estrogen-deficient state increases the risk of osteoporosis because estrogen is required to deposit calcium in bones and keep it there. Without sufficient estrogen, calcium loss from the bones speeds up. So you begin to miss out on one of the key hormones needed to maintain a healthy, strong bone structure. Menopause-related osteoporosis is technically known as Type I osteoporosis.

Scientists have recently discovered that early menopause spurs a greater decrease in bone density of the lower spine than either natural or premature menopause does. Premature menopause, however, results in lower bone density in the hip area than normal menopause does.

It's important to add that should you stop menstruating because of an eating disorder such as anorexia or bulimia, or because of excessive exercise, you may also lose bone more rapidly than normal.

YOU'RE SLIMMER THAN NORMAL

You've heard the expression "you can never be too thin or too rich." Wealth aside, you can most certainly be too thin. In fact, being thin and small boned puts you at serious risk of osteoporosis and increased risk of fracture—for four reasons:

- You have less trabecular bone, increasing the risk of fracture.

- You have less weight on your skeleton (which means there's not enough force applied to your bones to stimulate bone formation).

- You have less muscle and fat to pad and protect your bones from fracture.

- You tend to produce less bone-building estrogen after menopause.

How can you tell if you're "osteoporosis thin"? You might be considered thinner than usual if your body fat percentage is well under 10 percent, if you're an average-sized woman who weighs less than 127 pounds, or if you weigh less than you should for your body type.

By contrast, you're at less risk if you are overweight—for two possible reasons. First, extra weight may put more stress on the bones, and bone formation is stimulated when pressure is applied to bones. Second, fat cells produce bone-protective estrogen, thus offsetting the possible menopausal drop in that hormone.

The fact that being overweight reduces your risk does not give you an excuse to stay that way, nor a license to overeat. Although being overweight and obese are considered to be appearance problems, they are in fact serious conditions, directly linked to a number of disabling and life-threatening diseases. Among them: coronary heart disease, stroke, some cancers, diabetes, high blood pressure, gallbladder disease, osteoarthritis, and mental health problems.

After smoking, which causes an estimated 500,000 deaths a year, weight-related conditions are the second leading cause of death in the United States, claiming 300,000 lives each year. Thus, maintaining a not-too-thin, not-too-fat body is vital to overall health.

YOU'RE GETTING OLDER

With advancing age, bone integrity begins to deteriorate. Your bones become weaker and more porous, and your body becomes less efficient at absorbing calcium. Your risk of osteoporosis thus goes up.

Age-related bone loss is not well understood, however. Is it a side effect of aging, or is it aggravated by factors such as poor nutrition, hormonal deficiencies, or an inactive lifestyle? That's a question medical experts are still struggling to answer.

YOU'RE BEING TREATED FOR CERTAIN DISEASES

Osteoporosis is a complication of certain diseases and medical conditions, including thyroid disease, kidney disease, and high blood pressure.

Many physicians suggest that if you have hyperthyroidism—a condition caused by overproduction of the thyroid hormone thyroxine—get a bone mineral density test right away. Thyroxine accelerates your metabolism and, in doing so, may break bone down faster than the body can build it back up.

Hypothyroidism—underproduction of thyroxine— can take an indirect toll on bones too. The reason is that doctors prescribe synthetic thyroxine to treat hypothyroidism and if the dose is too high, the excess thyroxine will break down bones. If you're taking synthetic thyroxine, have your doctor monitor your dosage once or twice a year with a simple blood test.

In some people, kidney stones heighten the risk of osteoporosis. Diagnosed in more than one million people annually, kidney stones occur when calcium salts, uric acid, and other substances in urine crystallize to a form a hard, pebble-sized mineral pellet. Generally, people at risk of kidney stones excrete too much calcium, and become calcium deficient as a result. As a protective measure, the body dissolves bone to normalize its blood supply of calcium.

In addition, high blood pressure (hypertension), which affects 50 million Americans, may put you at risk of osteoporosis, particularly if you're a woman. That's the conclusion of a large-scale study conducted in Great Britain. The reason for the link, according to researchers, is that hypertensive patients excrete excessive amounts of bone-building calcium.

Other diseases associated with osteoporosis are listed in table 2.1.

YOU'RE TAKING CERTAIN PRESCRIPTION DRUGS

Osteoporosis can result from the prolonged use of certain drugs too. Among the major drug-culprits are

TABLE 2.1

Diseases Associated with an Increased Risk of Osteoporosis

Acromegaly	Fibromyalgia	Lymphoma
Addison's disease	Gastrectomy	Malabsorption problems
Amyloidosis	Gonadal insufficiency	Mastocytosis
Ankylosing spondylitis	Hemochromatosis	Multiple myeloma
Anorexia nervosa	Hemophilia	Multiple sclerosis
Biliary cirrhosis	Hyperparathyroidism	Nutritional disorders
Chronic obstructive	Hyperphosphatasia	Osteogenesis imperfecta
pulmonary disease	Hypertension	Pernicious anemia
Congenital porphyria	Hyperthyroidism	Rheumatoid arthritis
Cushing's syndrome	Idiopathic scoliosis	Sarcoidosis
Diabetes	Intestinal/bowel disease	Thalassemia
Endometriosis	Kidney disease	Thyrotoxicosis
Epidermolysis bullosa	Leukemia	

corticosteroids. In the body, corticosteroids are a group of steroid hormones secreted by the adrenal cortex, one of the adrenal glands. These hormones help the body resist stress caused by injury, illness, mental strain, severe exertion, and allergies. Without the adrenal cortex and its secretion of corticosteroids, your body would buckle under the potentially fatal effects of stress.

As medicine, synthetic corticosteroids are a class of powerful drugs used to treat various forms of inflammation and alleviate symptoms in a variety of disorders, including rheumatoid arthritis, severe asthma, and prevention of organ rejection from transplants. Some of the more common corticosteroids are hydrocortisone, prednisone, and prednisolone. They work by mimicking the actions of the natural hormones produced in the adrenal glands.

TABLE 2.2

Medications Associated with Osteoporosis

Anticonvulsants	GnRH
Chemotherapeutic drugs	Heparin
Corticosteroids	Lithium
Diuretics	Thyroxine (synthetic)

Trouble starts, however, because corticosteroids tamper with your body's ability to build new bone. Not only that, they impede the absorption of calcium by blocking the biochemical duties of vitamin D.

If you're taking corticosteroids, your physician may recommend that you fortify your diet with extra calcium. In addition, you may want to have a bone density test to check the state of your bones and make sure that corticosteroid therapy will not put you at further risk.

Inhaled steroids, prescribed for asthma, may lead to thinning bones, too. That's the finding of a just-published study that examined asthma sufferers who had been on inhaled steroids for six years. Researchers found that the patients had a significant loss of bone density and were at an increased risk of osteoporosis. If you use an inhaler, talk to your doctor about using the lowest possible dose that will control your asthma.

Another drug that breaks down bone too rapidly is gonadotropin-releasing hormone (GnRH), used to treat endometriosis. This disease develops when cells of the uterine migrate and grow elsewhere in the abdominal cavity. Although effective therapy for endometriosis, GnRH reduces reproductive capacity over time, reducing estrogen levels. When estrogen is in short supply, the body breaks down bone more rapidly.

Many other drugs can cause bone loss. These are

summarized in table 2.2. When osteoporosis accompanies disease or medication use, it is termed *secondary osteoporosis*. Treatment is tailored at curing the principal disease or discontinuing the offending drug.

YOU CAN'T STOMACH MILK

A little-known health risk associated with osteoporosis is a medical condition called lactose intolerance, a very common food sensitivity. People with lactose intolerance lack sufficient lactase, the enzyme required to digest lactose, a sugar in milk that helps you absorb calcium from the intestine. About 70 percent of world's population is lactose-intolerant. The condition causes a range of intestinal disturbances, from gas to severe pain and diarrhea.

If you have lactose intolerance, you may not consume enough calcium, a key mineral involved in bone health and strength. Even so, there are several options to ensure that you get all the calcium you need from milk and milk products. Try drinking small portions of milk (one-half cup at a time) at first to see if this amount can be tolerated. Also, aged cheeses and yogurts with active cultures may be better digested than straight milk.

Products such as enzyme-treated Lactaid milk, or Lactaid enzyme tablets for use at home, make milk consumption possible. Another enzyme product, Dairyease, is a tablet that, when taken before meals, assists with lactose digestion and lets you drink milk.

YOU'VE NEVER BEEN PREGNANT

If you've never been pregnant, you're at a slightly greater risk of osteoporosis. This is because pregnancy affects calcium balance in the body. When you're pregnant, levels of calcium rise in order to nourish the developing fetus. Repeated pregnancies can actually create a healthy oversupply of calcium in the body.

YOUR LIFESTYLE MAKES YOU PRONE TO OSTEOPOROSIS

Your health habits play a huge role in your chances of developing—or preventing—osteoporosis. Below we'll take a closer look at some of the lifestyle factors involved in this disease.

Low calcium intake

Calcium's best-known role in the body is as a builder of bones and teeth. In that capacity, it has a positive effect on osteoporosis. But if a dietary shortage exists, the body withdraws calcium from the storage vaults in the bone and dispatches it to the blood. The greater the draw, the more brittle the bones become. The potential for fractures increases, particularly in the spine, hip, and wrist, and the risk of osteoporosis climbs. (For more information on calcium, see chapter 8.)

Vitamin D deficiency

Vitamin D helps your body absorb calcium and is required for the breakdown and assimilation of phosphorus, a mineral involved in bone formation. So important is this vitamin to bone development that newborns properly nourished with vitamin D have stronger bones throughout life.

A prolonged deficiency of vitamin D causes osteomalacia (a bone-softening disorder better known as rickets) and hyperparathyroidism—two diseases that accelerate the development of osteoporosis. Deficiencies can be caused by poor nutrition and lack of adequate exposure to natural sunlight. Today, nearly all calcium supplements are fortified with vitamin D. (For more information on vitamin D, see chapter 8.)

A high-salt diet

Too much sodium in your diet can flush calcium from your body. What's more, high salt intake has been linked to the loss of an amino acid called hydroxyproline from bones. Hydroxyproline is the primary constituent of collagen, the major protein in bone tissue. Among medical experts, there is widespread consensus that restricting salt intake stops these losses and may help protect your bone.

High phosphorus consumption

Under normal conditions, the mineral phosphorus teams up with calcium to maintain a specific ratio of one part phosphorus to two parts calcium in bone. This ratio is needed for both minerals to be used properly by your body.

However, this balance can go awry, with the scales being tipped in favor of phosphorus. This imbalance is becoming more pronounced with the increased use of phosphorus-containing food additives. Eating too much phosphorus can interfere with the absorption of calcium, increasing the risk of osteoporosis. The recommended daily intake of phosphorus is 800 milligrams.

The major contributors of excess phosphorus to the diet are processed foods (which contain phosphates as preservatives), red meat, and soft drinks.

Excessive protein intake

Diets high in animal protein can cause calcium to leach out of the bones and not be reabsorbed, says a University of Texas study. The researchers added eggs and meat to the diets of vegans (vegetarians who eat no animal products) and observed that their risk of developing osteoporosis went up.

Another study looked at a group of Eskimos who eat up to 400 grams of protein a day (primarily from fish). Even though they get as much as 2,500 milligrams of calcium a day, their rate of bone loss and osteoporosis was much greater than that of Caucasian Americans.

What's more, red meat can block the absorption of calcium because of its high phosphorus content.

High caffeine consumption

If you drink a mugful of caffeinated coffee a day and don't take in enough calcium (under 600 milligrams a day), you're putting yourself in harm's way of getting osteoporosis. Research shows that coffee-drinking women with low-calcium diets have weaker bones and abnormally high losses of calcium in their urine.

In one study, a group of women, aged 22 to 30, who consumed 300 milligrams of coffee daily (the equivalent of about three cups) had double the normal loss of calcium in their urine for three hours after consumption.

Some good news, however: You can offset the negative effects of coffee by drinking a glass or two of milk every day. Or try drinking tea instead of coffee. For reasons not fully understood, tea drinking is associated with a decrease in hip fractures.

Alcohol abuse

Alcohol abuse endangers bone health in numerous ways. For example, alcohol:

- Interferes with the function of bone-forming osteoblasts, leading to impaired bone growth and poor bone density.

- Can damage the lining of the intestines, interfering with the normal absorption of calcium, vitamin D, and other bone-protective nutrients.

- Washes bone-friendly minerals (calcium, magnesium, and zinc) out of the body in urine.

In addition, alcoholics tend to eat diets that are low in calcium and other bone-building nutrients. Further, excessive alcohol increases their risk of falling and, with it, their susceptibility to fractures.

Scientifically, it has been verified that habitual, heavy drinking (100 grams of alcohol daily for more than ten years) can lead to osteopenia (low bone mass), which precedes osteoporosis.

Moderate alcohol usage (a few drinks weekly), however, does not seem to harm bone health and may even be associated with higher bone density in postmenopausal women, according to research. It's not clear why, however.

Inactivity

After astronauts go into space for any length of time, they lose bone mass because of the weightlessness of the environment. The same thing can happen to you if your bones and muscles aren't put to work, whether through inactivity (a sedentary lifestyle) or immobilization (confinement to bed due to illness or injury). If you're bedridden, you can lose as much as 1 percent of your trabecular bone per week.

In some ways, bones are like the plants in your house or yard. They will shrink due to neglect—which is why you must regularly move your body. Exercise and physical activity strengthen the skeleton by stimulating the bone to produce new cells.

Smoking

Cigarette smoking weakens bones in a number of ways. If you're a smoker (at least half a pack a day) or you breathe secondhand smoke on a regular basis, you could start menopause two years earlier than women who are nonsmokers. Premature menopause is a risk factor for osteoporosis. The probable reason for this is that smoking decreases the normal secretion of estrogen.

Smoking also interferes with your body's normal use of calcium and vitamin D, increasing the risk of osteoporosis.

In addition, smoking reduces your intake of oxygen, and oxygen is required for the proper functioning of all body cells. When oxygen is in short supply, bone cells can't properly manufacture bone, and you'll start losing bone as a result.

Smokers tend to be thinner than nonsmokers. As mentioned earlier, having a thin frame is a risk factor for osteoporosis.

Another red flag: Smoking in your youth is detrimental because it coincides with a period in your life when bone is still growing. Thus, if you smoked at a young age, you could have put your bones in jeopardy,

TABLE 2.3
Osteoporosis Risk Assessment

General

Are you female?

Are you Caucasian or Asian?

Are you small-boned, with a slender frame?

Are you older than 40 years of age?

Are you postmenopausal?

Did your menopause occur before age 45?

Have you experienced amenorrhea (loss or irregularity of periods) due to excessive exercise?

Family History

Do you have a family history of osteoporosis?

Has anyone in your family suffered a broken hip, shoulder, or wrist after age 45?

Medical History

Have you had any of the following illnesses or conditions?

- Thyroid disease
- Liver problems
- Kidney disease
- Rheumatoid arthritis
- Diabetes
- Part of stomach removed
- Bone fractures
- Intestinal disorders

Have you never been pregnant?

Have you been confined to bed for a long period of time?

Medication Use

Have you taken any of the following medications?

- Anticonvulsives
- Chemotherapy
- Diuretics
- GnRH
- Heparin
- Corticosteroids
- Thyroid medication

Nutrition

Is your diet low in milk and other dairy products?

Is your diet high in animal protein?

Do you eat a great deal of salty foods?

Are you a vegetarian who eats no milk or dairy products?

Are you lactose-intolerant?

Do you have an eating disorder?

Do you consume more than three cups of caffeinated coffee a day, or the equivalent?

TABLE 2.3 (continued)
Osteoporosis Risk Assessment

Exercise	Lifestyle
Do you exercise infrequently, or not at all?	Do you smoke cigarettes (at least half a pack a day)?
	Do you drink more than two alcoholic beverages a day?

since cigarette smoke damages bone cells and prevents bone growth.

Smoking during adulthood is linked specifically to lower bone density in the hip and lumbar spine (lower back). In fact, bone mineral density can decline by 5 to 10 percent in smokers. But no matter what age you are when you kick the habit, bone loss slows down from then on.

Are You at Risk?

With the exception of age, gender, ethnic background, and genetics, the risk factors for osteoporosis can be minimized or eliminated altogether. Unless you do so, you're putting your bone health on the line. To see if you could develop osteoporosis in the future, take the questionnaire in table 2.3. It will help you assess your risks. It is important to mention, however, that medical investigators believe that up to 35 percent of all women with no documented risk factors may develop osteoporosis.

Keep in mind, too, that this evaluation is only an awareness tool, and not meant to diagnose osteoporosis. The best way to determine bone health is to have your doctor look at your skeleton with a bone density test.

How did you score? The more times you answer yes
to the risk factors listed in the questionnaire, the higher
your risk—which should send you to your doctor's for
a bone density test.

3.

How Do I Know if My Bone Density Is Low?

With most illnesses or diseases, you know something is wrong because you have symptoms, those telltale warnings from your body that all is not well. But with osteoporosis, there are rarely any symptoms until the disease is quite advanced.

In fact, osteoporosis has been dubbed the "silent disease" because its signs appear so gradually that you hardly notice them. In many cases, osteoporosis gets overlooked, unless you have a bone density test to confirm it.

Even though bone loss keeps quiet, you must still listen to your body. There are a few warning signs to heed—signs that should warrant having a bone density test.

Physical evidence like the symptoms discussed below may point to the possibility that you have osteoporosis. But please don't self-diagnose. Only your doctor, using a bone density test, can tell for sure.

YOU'VE SUFFERED A FRACTURE

Unfortunately, the first sign of osteoporosis is often a fracture, usually in the hip joint, spine, or wrist. A fracture is a break in the bone and is by far the most serious symptom of osteoporosis. Each year, osteoporosis accounts for 500,000 spinal fractures and 300,000 hip fractures.

With osteoporosis, you can sustain a fracture by merely bending over to pick up a newspaper, pull weeds, or get up out of a chair. If their osteoporosis goes untreated, more than half of all Caucasian women will experience an osteoporotic fracture during their lifetime. Many who have one fracture will have others, because prior fractures are a risk factor for future fractures.

Other risk factors for osteoporosis-related fractures are:

- Low bone mass

- Low body weight

- Weight loss of 10 percent or more, beginning at age 50

- Recurrent falls, due to medications, poor vision, and poor mobility

- Lack of physical activity

- Inability to rise from a chair

- Medication use, particularly corticosteroids and sedatives

- Lifestyle factors such as smoking and alcohol abuse

- Dementia

- History of maternal fracture (hip)
- Poor general health

There are different types of osteoporotic fractures. All can have a devastating impact on your quality of life.

Vertebral (spinal) fractures
Your spine is supported by bones called vertebrae. There are seven vertebrae in the neck (cervical vertebrae); twelve at the back of the chest (thoracic vertebrae); and five in the lower back (lumbar vertebrae, or lumbar spine). The five lumbar vertebrae are depicted in figure 3.1.

The vertebrae are solid cylinders with a bony ring at the back through which the spinal cord passes. This ring also forms a protective passage for the spinal cord. Three spurs protrude from the ring to attach to the ribs and anchor the muscles of the back. The vertebrae are separated by rubbery cartilage disks, which allow the spine to bend. The disks are overlaid with collagen.

Spinal fractures are microscopic breaks in the vertebrae, brought on as the spine gradually deteriorates from age-related losses in bone mineral. More fractures occur in the vertebrae than anywhere else in the skeleton. One reason is that the spine is composed mostly of fracture-prone trabecular (inner layer) bone. However, spinal fractures almost never occur until you're age 50 or older. The risk of spinal fractures increases every year afterward.

Spinal fractures are difficult to diagnose because symptoms are either mild or nonexistent. Sometimes they're misdiagnosed as back strain.

Even so, many women experience pain from spinal

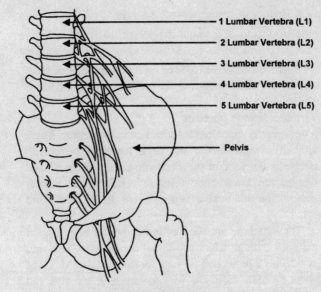

FIGURE 3.1
The lumbar spine is composed of five vertebrae.
L1 through L4 are the vertebrae measured in bone
density tests of the spine.

fractures. The pain ranges from mild to unbearable and
can persist for years. Chronic pain makes it hard to walk,
lift, do housework, and carry out other activities. Other
symptoms of spinal fractures include curvature of the
upper back and loss of height.

Your body remembers fractures. Having one spinal
fracture increases your odds of having another one and
of having a hip fracture. With multiple fractures, you're
more likely to suffer chronic disability.

Hip fractures

When doctors talk about a fracture in the hip, they're not referring to the pelvic bone, but rather to an area where the pelvis and femur (thighbone) come together at the hip joint. The hip joint is the largest and most stable joint in the body. Capable of bearing fifteen times its normal load, the hip joint is also the most stressed.

As figure 3.2 indicates, the femur is divided into the femoral head; the femoral neck; the femoral shaft, the long, uppermost portion of the thighbone; and two bony projections called the greater trochanter and the lesser trochanter. Located within the femoral neck is a site called Ward's triangle. Named after British osteologist Frederick O. Ward (1818–1877), Ward's triangle is very high in trabecular bone tissue.

The trochanters, which attach to muscles involved in hip movement, are frequently the site of osteoporotic fractures. Fractures commonly occur in the femoral neck too, as bones become more porous due to osteoporosis. As with spinal fractures, the risk of hip fracture increases with age.

Most hip fractures occur after a fall. Vitamin D deficiency, protein malnutrition, and other illnesses contribute to the likelihood of hip fracture, particularly in elderly women.

Hip fractures are life threatening. Tragically, women with a hip fracture are two to four times more likely to die within a year of the fracture, compared to women of the same age without a hip fracture. Death is often due to immobility following surgery. Immobility can lead to complications such as pneumonia and blood clots that may travel to the lungs.

In women surviving twelve months after suffering a hip fracture, independence and mobility decline signifi-

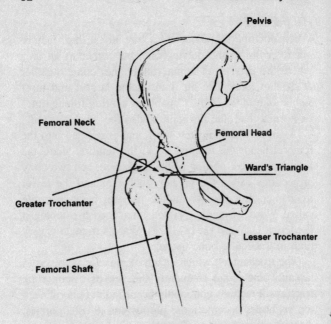

FIGURE 3.2
Hip fractures occur in an area where the pelvis and femur
(thigh bone) come together at the hip joint. This area is
evaluated in bone density tests of the hip. The femur is
divided into the femoral head, the femoral neck,
the femoral shaft, and the trochanters. A site called
Ward's triangle is located within the femoral neck.

cantly. In one study, up to 87 percent of women with
hip fractures never walked independently again. In another study, 31 percent of hip fracture survivors were
bedridden six years later.

Wrist and other fractures

With osteoporosis, you may break the bone just above your wrist. A fracture like this can keep you from doing household tasks, self-care, and other day-to-day activities.

Wrist fractures occur at a somewhat younger age than either spinal or hip fractures and thus can be a telltale sign of osteoporosis. In fact, a recent study says that if you fracture your wrist, you should be screened for osteoporosis—particularly if you're younger than 66 years old. A group of researchers in Scotland measured the bone density in thirty-one women, aged 40 to 82, who had sustained wrist fractures. These women were compared with women who had not suffered wrist fractures. Bone mineral density was lower in the fracture group—particularly among the 41- to 66-year-olds—than in the comparison group. The researchers concluded that women younger than age 66 who fracture their wrists should be "fully assessed for osteoporosis."

The odds of sustaining a wrist fracture increase rapidly after menopause, but unlike other fractures, drop off by 7 percent a year every year after age 60. The reason for this, according to medical theories, is that we tend to fall down or backward as we get older, rather than fall forward on our hands.

If you sustain a wrist fracture, you should definitely have a bone density test to confirm or deny the presence of osteoporosis.

Though somewhat less common, fractures of the pelvis, ribs, or jaw can occur as a result of osteoporosis.

YOU'RE SHRINKING

An early warning sign of bone loss is loss of height—at least one inch or more. Yearly measurements at your doctor's office are a good way to check for reduced height.

One of the chief causes of reduced height is an osteoporosis-related spinal fracture. When a bone in your spine fractures, it topples down on itself, causing you to lose some height. This may occur suddenly or gradually.

Spinal fractures are different from other osteoporotic fractures because they rarely produce any symptoms. They can be detected, however, with a bone density test.

But not all height loss can be blamed on osteoporosis. With age, the spongy cushions called disks between the vertebrae in the spine begin to degenerate and become less elastic. This loss of elasticity compresses your upper torso, shortening your height.

YOUR BACK HURTS

The pain may be severe, or dull and aching. If it doesn't go away with time and rest, chances are that you may have a spinal fracture brought on by osteoporosis. Spinal fractures occur when the bones in your back weaken, fracture, then collapse. They can happen suddenly, without warning—even when you sneeze or bend over.

YOUR UPPER BACK LOOKS ROUNDED

Multiple fractures brought on by osteoporosis can cause your spine to form a C curve. The resulting disfigurement is a dowager's hump, medically known as kyphosis. In this condition, the lower ribs impinge on the upper abdomen, and posture becomes stooped.

Because it is physically disfiguring, kyphosis can lead

to poor body image and, with it, emotional trauma such as depression. In other words, you don't like the way you look in the mirror—which hurts your self-esteem and self-confidence.

Depression brought on by poor body image is a double whammy. When you're depressed, your body churns out excess amounts of cortisol, a stress hormone that has been linked to bone loss.

With a flood of cortisol, your body really takes a beating. Your immune system begins to wear down, giving way to infections, illness, even brittle bones. In a study of bone density among twenty-six women (all in their forties), half the group suffered from depression, while the other half was emotionally stable. The depressed women had higher levels of stress hormones, including cortisol—and the bone density of 70-year-old women.

YOU'RE LOSING YOUR TEETH

Osteoporosis-related bone loss can also show up in your jaw. Usually the symptoms are loose teeth and frequent replacement of dentures due to bone loss and a receding jawbone.

YOU'RE PREMATURELY GRAY

Are you going gray? If so, your gray locks may be a sign of low bone density.

At least that's the conclusion of two studies conducted on the link between premature graying and bone loss. A study published in 1994 found that people with premature graying in their teens and twenties, but no other risk factors for osteoporosis, were 4.4 times as likely to have osteopenia than those without premature graying.

The other study, published in 1997, looked at 293 healthy postmenopausal women and found that those who turned gray in their twenties had lower overall bone density than those who went gray later in life.

Why the link between premature graying and low bone density? No one knows for sure, but some researchers think that the association could be due to genetic factors.

Diagnosing Osteoporosis

Taken together, your risk factors and any physical symptoms like those described above may be signs of bone trouble, and you should see your doctor for an accurate diagnosis. For starters, your physician will take a detailed family and medical history, which is usually the first step in making the diagnosis. Normally, you'll be asked about complaints of height loss, bone pain, change in posture, or other physical symptoms. Your family and medical history will also help your doctor sort out whether you are at risk for developing osteoporosis.

In addition to taking a family and medical history, your physician will conduct a thorough physical examination. During the exam, your physician will observe your stature and carriage and look for any signs of spinal curvature.

Health care professionals used to ask you for your height measurement. Increasingly, though, they now measure it themselves during routine physicals—for a number of reasons. One is that people typically underreport their height, just as they underreport their weight.

But the main reason is to check for progressive loss of height, which is a sign of osteoporosis. So for future reference, your height will be measured and compared to your tallest remembered height. In fact, expect your height to be routinely measured as a part of your annual physical. Keep in mind, though, that it is normal to lose roughly an inch of height as the disks in your spine age.

In older women, the physical examination may evaluate potential fall hazards, such as poor vision, the steadiness of your walk, and your ability to rise from a seated position.

If your physician believes that you may be at risk for osteoporosis, he or she will order a bone density test in order to arrive at a definitive diagnosis.

LABORATORY TESTS

Your physician may also order certain laboratory tests to exclude any secondary causes of osteoporosis. Below are the most common ones. In addition to these, your physician may order other, more specific lab tests.

Complete blood cell count (CBC)
This is a very common screening test that looks at the numbers and proportions of white blood cells and red blood cells in your body. Used to diagnose and manage diseases, CBC can find abnormalities in the manufacture and lifespan of blood cells, show problems in fluid volume such as dehydration, detect infections, or identify problems with blood clotting.

Chemistry panel (also called "blood chemistry group")
This is a blood test that examines levels of creatinine, electrolytes, alkaline phosphatase, and total protein and

albumin in your body. Used to evaluate kidney function, creatinine is a breakdown product of creatine, an energy-producing constituent of muscle. The kidneys excrete creatinine. When your kidneys are functioning normally, concentrations of creatinine in the blood remain constant and normal.

Electrolytes are minerals that help regulate fluid balance in body cells. The main electrolytes in extracellular fluid are sodium, calcium, and chloride, while in the intracellular fluid, the electrolytes are potassium, magnesium, and phosphorus. These nutrients provide a life-sustaining environment for all body cells and must be kept in proper balance. An imbalance can signal a medical problem.

Alkaline phosphatase is an enzyme found in all body tissues. Concentrations are particularly high in bone tissue. When tissue is damaged or diseased, alkaline phosphatase and other enzymes leak into the blood. Testing for alkaline phosphatase helps pinpoint the location of the damaged or diseased tissues. Abnormal values can be a sign of bone disease.

Measuring total protein in the blood can reveal a lot about your nutritional state, as well as the presence of kidney disease, liver disease, and many other conditions. The most highly concentrated protein in blood is albumin. Checking its level can determine if you have kidney or liver disease, or if your body is absorbing enough protein.

Thyroid-stimulating hormone (TSH)
Measuring levels of this hormone, which is produced by the pituitary gland, can detect the presence of thyroid disorders and diseases.

Sedimentation Rate

This test evaluates how fast red blood cells sink in a mass of drawn blood. If the cells sink faster than normal, this can mean infection or inflammation. The test can detect kidney disease, pregnancy, rheumatoid arthritis, thyroid disease, certain types of cancer, and a number of other illnesses.

Urinalysis

Most comprehensive medical exams include a urine test called a urinalysis. It looks for substances such as blood, sugar, and protein not normally present in urine. Detection of these substances may indicate a kidney disorder, an infection, a tumor, or other problems.

Toward a Definitive Diagnosis

Merely taking a medical history, performing a physical examination, and doing lab tests are not substitutes for bone density testing when diagnosing or evaluating your risk for osteoporosis. Thus, the next step in diagnosis is the bone mineral density test. Determining your level of bone mineral density helps your physician see where you stand in regard to osteoporosis, as well as make a definitive diagnosis.

At present, there are numerous such tests available. All of them are noninvasive, safe, and painless. No dyes are injected in any of these tests. The tests vary in the amount of radiation dose delivered.

Some machines measure "peripheral sites"—namely your fingers, wrists, or heel. Most of these devices are used as screening tools only, but are considered by the National Osteoporosis Foundation as acceptable for detecting osteoporosis. Usually, if a peripheral measurement indicates bone loss, your doctor will order a bone density test of your hip, spine, or both.

With the exception of ultrasound, all testing methods use absorptiometry. This means that they measure the amount of radiation absorbed into the bone being scanned. Absorptiometry uses small amounts of X rays to produce images of the spine, hip, or whole body. This technology is more sensitive than ordinary X rays because it can detect bone loss at an earlier stage. Normal X rays cannot detect bone loss until at least 30 percent of your bone has been depleted. X rays, however, can detect bone fractures.

Among the various types of tests, the dual-energy X-ray absorptiometry scan (DXA) is considered the standard. It gives your doctor a clear picture of the lumbar spine, hip, and other sites, and indicates how much calcium is in these areas. The DXA scan and other bone mineral tests are discussed in chapters 4 and 6.

4.

What Is a DXA Test?

If your doctor orders a bone density test, chances are it will be a dual-energy X-ray absorptiometry (DXA or DEXA) test. Available commercially since 1987, the DXA test is considered the "gold standard" for bone density measurement because it is the most accurate and advanced technique in use today. There are approximately five thousand DXA machines in the United States, and that number is growing.

DXA can detect bone loss in its earliest stages, predict fracture risk, help confirm a diagnosis of disease-related bone loss, and monitor changes in bone associated with therapy. It can also help you decide whether to pursue hormone replacement therapy (HRT), based on your degree of bone loss.

DXA is noninvasive and safe. It offers a relatively short scan time and low radiation exposure. There is no need even to worry about radiation. In fact, the exposure equals what you'd normally get from the environment in about one week or about one-tenth the normal radiation dose of a routine chest X ray.

How Accurate Is DXA?

When discussing the accuracy of DXA and other such tests, radiologists—physicians who specialize in the use of radiation energy to diagnose and treat disease—use the terms "sensitive," "specific," and "reproducible." "Sensitive" means that DXA can gauge loss of bone density very precisely. In fact, DXA is so sensitive that it can detect as little as two percent of bone loss a year.

"Specific" refers to DXA's ability to accurately estimate the true density of your bones. "Reproducible" means that results produced by the same machine are similar, several time periods apart.

Reproducibility and other accuracy factors are tested by using a "phantom." A phantom is a testing object that contains a known amount of calcium phosphate. Every three months on average, technologists scan the phantom with a DXA machine to ensure the accuracy of the machine, or to see whether it has deviated from its established standard of accuracy. Reproducibility is vital for achieving accuracy and precision and for monitoring the effects of therapy.

How Does DXA Work?

The DXA scanner emits two beams of very low level X rays passed over all, or part, of your body. The beams differ in strength: One is stronger than the other. Both are absorbed differently by your bones and soft tissue. The weaker beam, for example, is absorbed into soft tissue such as fat and muscle that surrounds the bones.

This subtracts the soft tissue out of the analysis so that bone can be isolated and its density assessed.

Density is measured by "counting" how bones absorb photons (bundles of atomic particles with no charge) that are generated by X ray machines. The result is a measurement that tells how much mineral occupies a particular quantity of bone.

Some scanners use "pencil-beam technology," which emits a tiny, narrowly focused beam that passes across a designated region in a rectangular pattern. The examination time per site with pencil-beam technology is from five to eight minutes. Full-body scanning requires about ten to twenty minutes.

Other devices use "fan-beam technology," often reserved for total body scans. Fan-beam units sweep over a designated area in a fan-shaped pattern and allow for more rapid scanning. Some machines can perform a whole body scan in less than five minutes. For health care institutions, fan-beam units are more expensive to buy. Typically, you'll find them at busier institutions where there is a very high turnover of patients being tested, and the cost can thus be justified. Both fan-beam technology and pencil-beam technology are comparable in terms of accuracy.

Which Sites Are Measured?

DXA machines measure bone density in "central" (also called "axial") sites. These refer to regions in the lumbar spine and in the hip, both of which are susceptible to fractures due to deteriorating bone density. Areas measured within the hip include the femoral neck, the trochanters, and Ward's triangle. The "shaft," which is the cylindrical uppermost portion of the thighbone, is measured too, but not normally used in the final estimation of bone density.

Using DXA technology, "peripheral" devices have been developed. Discussed in chapter 6, these devices measure bone density in outlying areas of the body, such as the forearm, wrist, fingers, and heel. Peripheral machines are used as initial screening tools for bone loss. Peripheral measurements, however, have not yet proven entirely useful for monitoring the effectiveness of osteoporosis treatments.

Ideally, your bone density should be measured at multiple sites. In all likelihood, your doctor will fill out a DXA request form that will include a choice of sites to be scanned. In most cases, scans of the spine and hip are routine. With the hip, either the left or right side may be measured.

How Should I Prepare for the Test?

No special preparations are required. Make sure, however, that you have the test performed at a major medical center, hospital imaging center, or physician's office where the radiologists and technologists have experience in doing bone density measurements.

Many radiologists have completed a certification course offered by the International Society for Clinical Densitometry. Radiologists are generally knowledgeable about preventive measures and treatments for osteoporosis.

Technologists who perform bone density tests are trained by the manufacturer of the testing equipment and are often certified by the International Society for Clinical Densitometry, as well.

Certain situations may postpone your DXA. These

include suspected pregnancy (be sure to inform your physician if you are pregnant), possibly, or a recent nuclear medicine scan such as a CT scan or X ray if an oral contrast agent was administered.

BEFORE YOUR DXA SCAN

You'll be asked to complete a detailed patient questionnaire, which is used by the radiologist in reporting back to your doctor. The questionnaire may request information on such items as:

- Age at first period
- Age at menopause
- Regularity or irregularity of periods
- Eating disorders
- Habits (smoking, alcohol usage, or caffeine usage)
- Surgical history, including hysterectomy
- Medication use
- Dietary calcium intake
- Use of calcium supplements
- Vitamin D intake
- Family history of osteoporosis
- Fall history
- Diseases
- Previous diagnosis of osteoporosis
- Fracture history

A sample questionnaire is shown in figure 4.1 at the end of this chapter.

Prior to your DXA test, you can eat or drink as you normally would. After arriving for your test, you will be asked by the technologist to remove any items on your clothing, such as buttons, buckles, zippers, keys, or coins that could interfere with the imaging process and cause inaccurate results.

The technologist will next record your height and weight, and possibly review your questionnaire with you. If you have not answered certain questions or failed to provide enough information, the technologist may interview you at that time to fill in any gaps.

DURING YOUR DXA SCAN

You will be asked to lie on your back on a scanning table that is approximately six to eight feet long. Foam positioning aids will be placed under and around parts of your body to ensure that the images taken will be clear.

Lie still, breathe normally, and relax. An imager will pass back and forth over your body to be scanned, taking images of the bones in your hip, spine, or forearm—particularly their calcium content.

If your lumbar spine (lower back) is being examined, for example, your hips and knees will be flexed over a support. This position helps align your spine and keeps it flat against the table. The technologist will make sure that your spine is centered and straight.

When your hip region is scanned, your leg is slightly turned and rotated with the use of a positioner for better precision. For whole body scanning, all parts of your body will be included in the scan field.

Correct positioning is important for obtaining an accurate measurement of bone density. It is the technologist's responsibility to ensure that your body is in the proper position during the test. Be sure to lie very still, however, since movement during the scan can affect the results.

The DXA scan is painless and comfortable, and takes five to fifteen minutes. If you suffer from back pain, however, you may feel uncomfortable while lying motionless on the scanning table.

AFTER YOUR DXA SCAN

After your scan is over, you may need to wait a few minutes so that the technologist can review your images to make sure that the regions of interest were properly scanned.

Software that comes with the DXA machine prints out scan data. Generally, most DXA machines print out the following information:

- An image of the region that was scanned.

- A graph that plots your bone mineral density for that region against your age.

- Numerical data that summarize your findings. (For more information on this data, see chapter 5.)

The technologist gives the radiologist your completed questionnaire, any prior X rays or scans you've had, and the DXA printouts. The radiologist carefully reviews each item before writing or dictating a report to your doctor.

Normally, the final results are available in a few days

and will be sent to your personal physician. There are no special precautions to take following your test.

Are There Any Drawbacks to a DXA Scan?

Spinal measurements can be slightly inaccurate due to degenerative changes caused by osteoarthritis, scoliosis, bone spurs, or other skeletal irregularities. These can falsely elevate your bone mineral density and produce misleading results.

Radiologists, however, are trained to spot degenerative changes on the image printed out by the DXA machine. These changes usually appear as darkened areas on the image. If your scan shows degenerative changes on one vertebra, for example, the radiologist will use information from the normal vertebrae to assess your bone density.

In addition, there are DXA machines capable of taking lateral scans of the spine. These devices are supposed to allow easier identification of spinal abnormalities that could skew the results. Some radiologists, however, do not feel that these machines are effective in this regard.

How Much Does a DXA Scan Cost?

The test costs anywhere from $150 to $300. It is not always covered by insurance, except in certain cases.

In 1998 the Bone Mass Measurement Act was passed in Congress, ensuring Medicare coverage for bone density testing for the following patients:

- Estrogen-deficient women at clinical risk of osteoporosis. According to physicians Carolina Kulak and

John P. Bilezikian, writing in the *International Journal of Fertility and Women's Medicine*, "Although the regulation is somewhat ambiguous on this point, it is reasonable to expect that these estrogen-deficient subjects at risk include those with a family history of osteoporosis, low body weight, history of anorexia, amenorrhea [loss of periods] for at least one year during the reproductive years, diseases associated with bone loss, and certain medications."

▪ People with vertebral abnormalities

▪ People receiving long-term corticosteroid therapy (specifically more than 7.5 milligrams of prednisone a day for longer than three months)

▪ Individuals with primary hyperparathyroidism

▪ Individuals being monitored to assess the effectiveness of an FDA-approved drug for osteoporosis therapy

In addition, Medicare will reimburse for bone density tests only when they are ordered by your physician, and the frequency of testing is once every two years. Other insurers may vary in their coverage.

Having a bone density test to screen for osteoporosis, or to establish a baseline, may not be covered by your health insurance, and you may thus have to foot the bill. However, the test may be reimbursable if it is ordered to evaluate or diagnose possible bone disease rather than as a screening test. Check with your insurance agent or health care provider.

When Should I Have Another Test?

Based on recommendations from the radiologist, your physician will decide when you should have your next test, and at what intervals. Usually, tests are repeated at intervals of one or two years. It may be sooner, however, if you take medications that can degrade bone, have had an organ transplant, or suffer from a disease that affects bone. In these cases, you might be scheduled for a test after an interval as short as six months.

If possible, you should be tested on the same machine. Results are not always comparable ("reproducible") between machine brands because different manufacturers use different measurement methods.

FIGURE 4.1

Example of a patient questionnaire

This questionnaire was provided as a courtesy by
St. Mary's Breast Center in Evansville, Indiana.

BONE DENSITY HISTORY SHEET

Date: _____ Referring Physician: _____

Name: _____

Age: _____ Height: _____ Weight: _____

Previous Bone Mineral Density Study? Yes _____ No _____

If yes, where? _____

Family history of bone fracture in your mother or sister?

Yes _____ No _____

Do you smoke? Yes _____ No _____

Do you still have menstrual periods? Yes _____ No _____

If no: menopause age _____

Do you have spine pain? Yes _____ No _____

Have you had loss of height? Yes _____ No _____

Number of alcoholic drinks per week: _____

Servings of dairy products per day: _____
    (milk, cheese, yogurt, ice cream, etc.)

Hours of weight-bearing exercise per week: _____

Medical history: check all that apply to you

_____ Addison's disease (adrenal insufficiency)

_____ Smoking-related lung disease (emphysema)

_____ Endometriosis

_____ Hyperparathyroidism
_____ Insulin-dependent diabetes
_____ Multiple myeloma
_____ Rheumatoid arthritis

Medications: check all medications you currently take
_____ Seizure medication
_____ Steroids
_____ Tamoxifen (Nolvadex)
_____ Evista (Raloxifene)
_____ Fosamax (Alendronate)
_____ Miacalcin (Calcitonin)
_____ Hormone replacement therapy
_____ Calcium supplements

5.

How Do I Interpret My Results?

The results of the DXA and other bone density tests are usually reported in three different types of documents, produced in the following order:

1. *A printout generated by the software that comes with the testing equipment.* This document contains a series of numbers and other data used to determine the health of your bones. (Depending on the testing facility, you may or may not get a copy of this report.)

The printout is first analyzed and interpreted by a radiologist. It is the radiologist's job to analyze the scan data accurately and report his or her findings to your physician.

(For an explanation of the components of this printout, refer to the discussion below.)

2. *The radiologist's report.* After analyzing the printout and interpreting the data, the radiologist provides

your physician with a clinically useful report. In that report, the radiologist will note your scores for the sites measured and indicate whether your bone density is normal, in the low normal range, or significantly below normal.

Usually, the radiologist's report includes comments on technical aspects of the scan, including any skeletal abnormalities that were detected. Reports are generally tailored to the preferences of your doctor, who will use it to make decisions regarding your treatment.

3. *A letter from your physician.* Using the radiologist's report, your physician will probably draft a letter to you explaining your results. In some cases, this letter may come directly from the testing facility.

If you completed a questionnaire on risk factors prior to your bone density test, the letter may list your top four risk factors. The letter may also give recommendations for calcium and vitamin D intake, exercise, and drug therapy. An example of a letter is shown in figure 5.1.

Finally, the letter may recommend that you have a repeat DXA test at certain intervals, depending on what your test results reveal. In addition to writing a letter, your physician should personally discuss your results with you.

Understanding the Numbers

You can request a copy of the report printed out by the testing equipment. (Figure 5.2 shows an example of a DXA-generated report.) Should you receive a copy, it's important to understand what its numbers mean. Keep in mind that bone density reports vary somewhat

FIGURE 5.1
Sample letter from a testing facility to a 69-year-old
female patient

Dear _____ :

It was a pleasure having you as a patient on _____ .
Your bone density (DEXA) scan revealed you have 72% of the
normal bone density of the young adult reference population
in the lumbar spine, 77% of the normal bone density of the
young reference population in the hip, and 87% of the normal
bone density of the young adult reference population in the
wrist. These values are consistent with osteoporosis. Your current risk for fracture is increased 6 times for the spine, 3.5 times
for the hip, and 3 for the wrist, based on your bone density
measurement alone.

Additional risk factors include:

> Female
> Caucasian
> Postmenopausal
> Prior smoking history

I recommend that you discuss these findings with your physician, as well as possible risk factor modifications or treatment
plans.

Possible treatments might include:

> Exercise program
> Dietary calcium supplement
> Hormonal supplement
> Calcitonin
> Fosamax
> Evista

Thank you for choosing _____ as a participant
in your ongoing health care.

Sincerely,

Physician's name

in how they present information. This is because different types of scanning devices generate different types of
reports. All reports, however, are technical documents
that include these basic categories of information:

- *Patient biographical information.* This generally
includes your name, age, birth date, height, weight,
race, and sex.

- *A computerized image of each site scanned.* This
helps the radiologist detect any skeletal abnormalities
that may affect bone density measurements.

- *A list of each site that was evaluated.* For example,
if your femur was scanned, the report will list such
sites as femoral neck, Ward's triangle, and the greater
trochanter. DXA may also give a bone density measurement for the total hip.
    Likewise, a scan of your lumbar spine gives in-
dividual bone density measurements for each vertebra
(listed on the report as L1, L2, L3, and L4).

- *The bone area measured at specific sites.* With
DXA, area is measured and expressed as centimeters
squared, because the test produces two-dimensional
images. (Some tests measure volume; these are explained in the next chapter.)

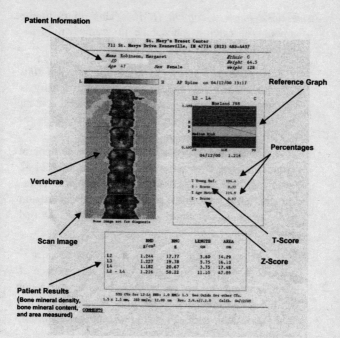

Patient Information

Reference Graph

Percentages

Vertebrae

Scan Image

T-Score

Z-Score

Patient Results
(Bone mineral density,
bone mineral content,
and area measured)

FIGURE 5.2
Printed reports from DXA machines can be broken
down into these major areas: patient biographical
information, scan image, reference graph, and bone
measurement results (including T-score, Z-score, and
percentages). This report gives the results for a bone
density test of the lumbar spine.

- *Bone mineral content (BMC).* This refers to the amount of calcium phosphate in grams within selected sites of your bone.

- *Bone mineral density (BMD) within selected sites of your bone.* With DXA, bone mineral density is calculated by dividing grams of bone mineral content by the bone area (in centimeters squared) and is reported as grams per square centimeter.

Let's say, for example, that the total bone mineral content scanned by DXA in your femur was 24.42 grams and the area scanned was 30.21 square centimeters. Your bone mineral density in the hip region is 0.808 grams per centimeter squared (24.42 divided by 30.21).

- *A reference graph on which your bone density is plotted.* The graph compares you to other women of your same age group, race, height, and weight. A dot on the graph indicates where you fall in comparison and states your level of risk in terms of low, medium, or high.

- *Your T-score and Z-score.* These values express your bone mineral density in relation to "reference populations." A reference population comes from thousands of ambulatory (able to walk) female subjects with no history of chronic disease affecting bone, no medications affecting bone, and no history of nonviolent fractures. T-scores and Z-scores are discussed in detail below.

- *Percentages.* Bone mineral density is also reported in percentages in relation to a reference population. Percentages are generally easier to comprehend than T-scores and Z-scores are.

Reports usually contain two percentages for each site measured. One percentage (the one paired with your T-score) indicates whether your bone density is above or below average for peak bone density (achieved by age 30). This percentage is also called the "young adult percentage" (YA). For example:

- If your YA percentage is 100 percent, your bone mineral density is equal to that of the average 30-year-old woman.
- If you get a score, say, of 115 percent, your bones are in even greater shape.
- If your score is 75 percent, it's time to start some bone-saving measures.

The second percentage (the one paired with your Z-score) indicates whether your bone density is above or below average for your age.

The percentages of each site are averaged to provide a total percentage. Examples of typical analyses are shown in tables 5.1 through 5.4 in this chapter.

What Do My T-Score and Z-Score Mean?

After the scan is over, the bone density test compares the amount of mineral in your bones with two norms, or standards, called age-matched (Z-score) and young-normal (T-score). Technically, these numbers are a statistical measurement called a standard deviation. A standard deviation equals about 10 to 12 percent and describes how far above or below a norm you fall.

UNDERSTANDING YOUR Z-SCORE

Normally, you lose bone density with age. Your Z-score is a numerical reading that expresses how your bone density stacks up against the average bone density for a healthy person your same age. It can help a doctor detect whether conditions other than aging or osteoporosis have triggered bone loss. It is not used to make a diagnosis of osteoporosis, however.

A negative value is a sign that you have thinner bones (lower bone density) than other women in your same age group. Let's say, for example, that you're 60 years old and your Z-score in your femur is -2.0. That means you've lost more bone in that area than women in your same age bracket. Chances are, other factors besides age and menopause are causing your bones to crumble. Disease or medication may be the culprits.

A Z-score below -2 is considered to be a significant indicator of risk. On the other hand, a positive value shows that you have more bone density than other women in your age group.

UNDERSTANDING YOUR T-SCORE

What counts most is the T-score. It is a numerical comparison to the average bone density found at peak bone mass (usually achieved by age 30).

Your T-score indicates whether your bones are more dense ($+$), less dense ($-$), or the same density as the bones of a healthy 30-year-old woman, which is a T-score of 0.

Here's a look at how to interpret your T-score, based on definitions established by the World Health Organization (WHO) in 1994. These criteria are widely accepted throughout the world:

- Normal bone density is any T-score between $+1$ and -1.

- Low bone mass, or osteopenia, is a T-score between −1 and −2.5.

- Osteoporosis is a T-score at or below −2.5. Women in this group who have already suffered one or more fractures are diagnosed as having severe (or established) osteoporosis.

Your T-score provides valuable medical information. Based on your T-score, your physician can recommend specific preventive actions and/or prescribe anti-osteoporosis medicines to halt the progression of bone loss. Chapter 7 takes a closer look at some of the preventive and prescriptive measures recommended on the basis of T-scores in specific periods of life. T-scores, however, are not the sole determinants of treatment decisions.

How Your Fracture Risk Is Determined

T-scores are used to compute fracture risk because risk increases as bone mineral density declines from peak bone density at age 30, otherwise known as the young adult reference value. In practical terms, if you score much lower than an average young adult woman, your odds of sustaining a fracture climb substantially.

For each standard deviation of bone density below the young adult mean, fracture risk generally increases by 2-fold. (Some osteoporosis experts say that risk increases by 1.5- to 3-fold.)

Bone specialists Leon Lenchik, Paul Rochmis, and David J. Sartoris used the following example in the *American Journal of Roentgenology* to explain how risk is calculated:

Mathematically, risk computes according to the following formula: relative risk $= 2^{|T\text{-score}|}$. Let's say, for example, that you're 57 years old, with a spinal T-score of -4.0 (four standard deviations below the norm).

Your risk of spinal fracture is $2^{|-4.0|}$ (2^4, or $2 \times 2 \times 2 \times 2$). This computation equals 16. Thus, you have approximately sixteen times the risk of fracture that healthy young adults have.

My DXA Scan

Because I'm approaching menopause (I'm 48), I asked my personal physician to order a DXA scan. That way, I would have a baseline measurement for future bone density tests.

Prior to the test, I had to sign a waiver. It explained that some insurance companies do not pay for routine bone mass measurement tests. By signing the waiver, I agreed that I would pay the testing facility for the scan if my insurance company did not reimburse me.

Next, I completed a patient questionnaire like the one shown in the previous chapter.

The technologist escorted me to a small, dimly lit room where there was a DXA scanner and a computer. She instructed me to lie on my back on the cushioned scanning table with my legs draped over a large cube-shaped positioner. She entered my name, Social Security number, age, sex, race, height, and age into the computer.

The technologist scanned my spine first. Over the course of about five minutes, an overhead scanning arm advanced across my torso in short movements while making a low whirring noise. After the spinal scan was over, a vivid digitized image of my spine, along with various data, appeared on the computer screen.

To perform the hip scan, the technologist removed the positioner and placed another positioner between my legs. She then strapped my legs against the positioner in such a way that my feet were pigeon-toed. The scanning arm advanced across my hip region in short movements. The scan took less than five minutes, and an image of my hip region appeared on the computer screen.

The results of both scans were available within about ten minutes of the test. This particular facility issues a letter to patients, describing the results. My letter stated: "Compared to the normal peak bone mass, you have normal bone mass. Please follow up with your physician regarding your test results." A few weeks later, I received a brief letter from my personal physician, confirming that my bone density is normal.

I asked for a copy of the DXA scan report printed out by the machine. The radiologist obliged, although these printouts are normally sent to the referring physician and not often given to patients.

Being familiar with the data and terminology helped me make sense of my results. Both scans featured graphs that plotted my bone mineral density scores in the low-risk category.

My spinal T-score was 0.32; my young adult percentage was 104.4, which is 4.4 percent above the average for peak bone density. Both numbers indicate that my vertebrae are healthy—even slightly stronger than those of a 30-year-old woman.

My spinal Z-score was 0.97; my age-matched percentage was 114.9, indicating that my bone density is above average for my age.

As for my hip, my T-score was 0.01, reflecting normal bone density. My young-normal percentage was 100.1, which means that the bone density in my hip matches that of an average 30-year-old woman. My Z-score was 0.84, and my age-matched percentage was 111.1, a sign that my bones are more dense than most women my age.

I attribute this healthy report primarily to exercise. Since 1980, I have lifted weights regularly—at least three to four times a week. Weight-training is one of the best physical activities for stimulating the formation of new bone. In addition, I have always followed a healthy diet, one that has included plenty of calcium-rich foods.

Examples of Typical Analyses

Table 5.1 shows the results of a DXA scan of a 79-year-old woman's lumbar spine.

The first column notes the region scanned—the four vertebrae of the lower spine. The second column gives the size (in centimeters squared) of the area scanned. These values are added together to provide a sum total.

The third column lists the amount of bone mineral content present at the specific sites that were measured. Bone mineral content values are added together to provide a sum total.

Bone mineral content is divided by the area to determine bone mineral density (fourth column). Her bone mineral density value for the four vertebrae is 1.188, calculated by 44.99/37.88. In the fifth and sixth columns, the results for each vertebra are compared with the young adult normal population (T-score) and with an age-matched population (Z-score). This woman's T-score for her lumbar spine is 0.1, the average of the T-scores for vertebrae L1 through L4. Her Z-score is 2.4, the average of the Z-scores for vertebrae L1-L4.

The percentages for the T-score and Z-scores of each

TABLE 5.1

**Lumbar spine measurements made from a DXA scan
of a 128-pound white female, age 79**

Region Scanned	Area (cm²)	Bone Mineral Content (grams)	Bone Mineral Density (grams/cm²)	T-Score SD*	T-Score %	Z-Score SD*	Z-Score %
L1	9.95	8.93	.897	−1.9	79	0.4	105
L2	9.14	11.41	1.248	0.4	104	2.7	135
L3	8.47	11.24	1.327	1.1	111	3.4	144
L4	10.32	13.41	1.299	0.8	108	3.1	141
(L1–L4)	37.88 (Total)	44.99 (Total)	1.188 (44.99 ÷ 37.88)	0.1 (Average of L1–L4)	101 (Average % of L1–L4)	2.4 (Average of L1–L4)	131 (Average % of L1–L4)

(Scan data provided by Methodist Hospital, Henderson, Kentucky.)
*Standard deviation units. The totals in the fifth and sixth columns are averages of L1, L2, L3, and L4.

vertebra are averaged to provide single percentages. In
this example, her total bone mineral density (101%) is
one percent above the average (100 + 1 = 101) for peak
bone density of a normal young adult and thirty-one percent above the average for age (100 + 31 = 131). Based
on these measurements, this woman has normal bone
density in her lumbar spine.

Table 5.2 shows the results of a DXA scan on the same
woman's femur. The first column lists the five regions
that were scanned. Included in this list is an overall value
for the hip, referred to as "total hip." In most cases, the
regions given the highest consideration by radiologists
are the femoral neck and total hip because most fractures
occur there. Other regions such as Ward's triangle are
considered less precise and not usually figured in bone
density scores.

The second column gives the size (in centimeters
squared) of the five areas scanned. The third column lists
the amount of bone mineral present at the five sites that
were measured.

Bone mineral content is divided by the area to determine bone mineral density (fourth column).

In the fifth and sixth columns, the results of each site
measured are compared with the young adult normal
population (T-score) and with an age-matched population (Z-score). In this example, the woman's T-score is
−1.6, based on femoral neck and total hip measurements. Her Z-score is 0.3, based on her total hip measurement.

Her young adult and age-matched percentages are
also based on her total hip measurement. In this example, her bone mineral density (81%) is 19 percent below
the average (100 − 81 = 19) for peak bone density of

TABLE 5.2

Shows the same woman's left femur measurements

Region Scanned	Area (cm²)	Bone Mineral Content (grams)	Bone Mineral Density (grams/cm²)	T-Score SD*	T-Score %	Z-Score SD*	Z-Score %
Neck	4.60	3.60	0.782	−1.6	80	0.4	107
Ward's	2.35	1.45	0.617	−2.3	68	0.3	107
Trochanter	12.51	7.19	0.575	−2.0	73	−0.5	91
Shaft	13.10	13.63	1.040	–	–	–	–
Total Hip Area	30.21	24.42	0.808	−1.6	81	0.3	105

(Scan data provided by Methodist Hospital, Henderson, Kentucky.)
*Standard deviation units. The totals in the fifth and sixth columns are averages of the neck, Ward's triangle, and trochanter.

TABLE 5.3

Lumbar spine measurements made from a DXA scan of a 57-year-old postmenopausal woman who is not receiving hormone replacement therapy

Region Scanned	Bone Mineral Density (grams/cm²)	T-Score SD*	%	Z-Score SD*	%
L1	0.643	−4.1	57	−2.9	65
L2	0.725	−4.0	60	−2.8	68
L3	0.717	−4.0	60	−2.9	67
L4	0.705	−4.1	59	−3.0	66
Average of L1–L4	0.700	−4.0	59	−2.9	67

Scan data adapted from: Lenchik, L., P. Rochmis, and D. J. Sartoris, 1998. Optimized interpretation and reporting of dual X-ray absorptiometry (DXA) scans. *AJR* 171:1509–1520.
*Standard deviation units. The totals in the third and fourth columns are averages of L1, L2, L3, and L4.

a normal young adult and 5 percent above the average for age (100 + 5 = 105).

This particular woman would be considered mildly osteopenic in her femur.

Table 5.3 shows a 57-year-old woman's lumbar spine measurements.

The analysis of her spine from L1 to L4 shows that the T-score is −4.0 and the Z-score is −2.9. In this example, the total spinal bone mineral density (59%) is 41 percent below the average (100 − 59 = 41) for peak bone density of a normal young adult and 33 percent below the average for age (100 − 67 = 33).

TABLE 5.4

Femur measurements made from a DXA scan of a 57-year-old postmenopausal woman who is not receiving hormone replacement therapy

Region Scanned	Bone Mineral Density (grams/cm²)	T-Score		Z-Score	
		SD*	%	SD*	%
Neck	0.705	−2.3	72	−1.3	82
Ward's	0.508	−3.1	56	−1.7	70
Trochanter	0.536	−2.3	68	−1.8	73
Shaft	0.808	−	−	−	−
Hip Area	0.683	−2.4	68	−1.7	75

Scan data adapted from: Lenchik, L., P. Rochmis, and D. J. Sartoris, 1998. Optimized interpretation and reporting of dual X-ray absorptiometry (DXA) scans. *AJR* 171:1509–1520.
*Standard deviation units.

* * *

Table 5.4 shows the results of a DXA scan on the same woman's femur.

This example lists the five sites that were scanned. Her total hip measurement is used to determine her T-score (−2.4) and her Z-score (−1.7). Here, her bone mineral density is 32 percent below the average (100 − 68 = 32) for peak bone density of a normal young adult and 25 percent below the average for age (100 − 75 = 25).

Of interest in comparing both scans is the more noticeable loss of spinal bone density as compared to bone loss in the hip. The vertebrae are composed of mostly trabecular bone, whereas the hips are made up of mostly cortical bone. These scans reflect what commonly happens to your bones following menopause, particularly if you're not on HRT: more extensive loss of trabecular bone in the spine, compared to less loss of cortical bone in the hip.

This woman would be considered osteoporotic in her spine, but osteopenic in her hip.

6.

Are There Other Tests?

In addition to DXA, other types of tests measure bone density—and do so in different ways. Some measure peripheral, or outlying, areas of the skeleton, such as the heel or forearm; others measure "central" areas of the skeleton, such as the spine or hip. DXA, which was discussed in chapter 4, is a central test. There are also peripheral DXA tests.

Some of the tests discussed in this chapter are used as screening tools only. Depending on the results provided by a screening test, your doctor may recommend that you have a DXA test.

There may be slight variations in the accuracy of each test, but generally, the methods discussed below are reliable, with the ability to detect the impact of age, menopause, and other factors on bone density.

It is thus important to be aware of the differences in these tests and how they are used. Also, if a DXA test is not available in your area—and you want to know your bone density—other tests may be more accessible. A comparison of the major tests now in use is presented in table 6.1 on pages 88–90.

This chapter describes twelve methods used to measure bone density. These are grouped according to: (1) central bone density measurements, (2) peripheral bone density measurements, and (3) biochemical bone markers. Also discussed is magnetic resonance imaging (MRI), considered an emerging technology in the field of bone densitometry.

Central Bone Density Measurements

DPA (DUAL PHOTON ABSORPTIOMETRY)

What is it?
Introduced in the 1960s, DPA is the predecessor to DXA. DPA has been used to measure bone density in the spine, hip, and whole body.

How does it work?
DPA uses a double beam from a radioactive energy source called a photon to measure bone density. The DPA test is now in limited use, however.

How accurate is it?
DPA has numerous drawbacks, including poor precision and long scan times. Scanning the entire body by DPA takes forty to sixty minutes. It is difficult for patients to remain still that long. As a result, patient movement can affect the accuracy of the test.

How much does the test cost?

The cost ranges from $150 to $300. Except for use in research studies, DPA is rarely used. It has been replaced by the more technologically advanced DXA.

QCT (QUANTITATIVE COMPUTED TOMOGRAPHY)

What is it?

QCT uses a conventional computed tomography (better known as a CT scan), along with special hardware and software. All forms of computed tomography combine X rays with computer technology to provide clear images of tissue in greater detail than ordinary X rays.

QCT looks at bone in three dimensions and thus measures *volumetric density* of bone. This describes the mass of minerals within a defined *volume* of bone. The results of QCT are expressed in grams per centimeters cubed (g/cm^3).

By contrast, other tests such as DXA are two-dimensional and thus measure bone *area*. The results of these tests are given as grams per centimeter squared (g/cm^2), described as *areal density*.

QCT is primarily a diagnostic tool, rather than a screening device, for assessing bone density in the spine. Newer QCT machines have been developed with the capability of measuring bone density in the hip.

How does it work?

As with most CT scans, you disrobe and then lie on a movable scanning table that is guided through the tunnel of the CT scanner. X rays are then beamed through segments of the body and picked up by detectors. This information is read by a computer that converts it into an image that can be interpreted by a radiologist.

The procedure takes ten to fifteen minutes. Like the DXA scan, results are reported as T-scores.

A drawback to QCT is that it emits the highest radiation dose of all bone mineral tests. It may also be more costly.

How accurate is it?

QCT is accurate, particularly for measuring trabecular bone in the spine. It has been used to assess the risk of spinal fractures, measure age-related bone loss, and monitor patients in both clinical practice and research studies. QCT is used at more than four thousand centers worldwide.

Even so, many radiologists remain unconvinced about QCT's usefulness. Anthony Perkins, M.D., chairman of the Department of Radiology at Methodist Hospital in Henderson, Kentucky, explained, "We had QCT in our hospital, but were concerned about its accuracy and reproducibility. Based on my personal experience, I believe that QCT overestimated the degree of bone mineral loss. We have since started using DXA."

How much does the test cost?

The cost of QCT ranges from $150 to $400 for a measurement of the spine.

Peripheral Bone Density Measurements

SXA (SINGLE-ENERGY X-RAY ABSORPTIOMETRY)

What is it?

SXA has been employed to measure bone density in the Apollo astronauts. It emits a single beam of radiation to assess bone density in the forearm or the heel. The heel is measured in various types of bone density tests because its composition is similar to that of the spine. Aided by a formula, heel measurements can be used to predict bone density in the spine.

Some bone specialists, however, frown on the practice of using measurements of the heel, or other sites, to predict measurements in other regions of the body.

Writing in the *Journal of Bone and Mineral Research*, Michael Kleerekoper, M.D., a leading bone specialist, commented: "If you want to know the bone mineral density of the hip, measure it at the hip, not the spine and predict it from a formula."

How does it work?

With SXA, you sit comfortably in a chair and place your limb in a water bath. The water bath helps the X ray discriminate between bone and soft tissue. If your forearm is being scanned, you grasp a vertical rod. If your heel is scanned, you place your foot in a small, open unit. Forearm scanning takes approximately five minutes; heel scanning, about two minutes.

Whenever the forearm is scanned, the technologist will ask you whether you're right- or left-handed. If you're right-handed, your left (nondominant) forearm will be scanned, and vice versa.

How accurate is it?

SXA is highly accurate. Although DXA is considered the "gold standard" in testing, SXA has performed favorably in comparison. Case in point: In a study conducted in Thailand, researchers measured the bone mineral density of 325 healthy women who were patients at a menopause clinic. The researchers used DXA to evaluate bone mineral density in the hip and spine, and SXA to assess the forearm. SXA measurements of the forearm correlated well with DXA measurements of the hip and spine.

Nonetheless, bone specialists generally agree that results obtained from any type of heel scan should be confirmed with a DXA scan.

How much does the test cost?
The test costs between $50 and $150.

SINGLE PHOTON ABSORPTIOMETRY (SPA)

What is it?
First introduced in 1963, single photon absorptiometry (SPA) is an earlier generation of SXA. It has been used to measure trabecular and cortical bone in the forearm and to predict fracture risk in the skeleton, hip, and spine.

How does it work?
SPA uses a single beam from an energy source that passes through water. SPA emits very low doses of radiation and takes approximately fifteen minutes.

How accurate is it?
SPA is not as accurate as other, more technologically advanced bone density tests. One problem with SPA is that it does not do a good job of discriminating between bone and soft tissue.

How much does the test cost?
The cost ranges from $50 to $150. However, SPA is not employed very much anymore because of its limitations in accuracy. It has been replaced by SXA and DXA.

PERIPHERAL QUANTITATIVE COMPUTED
TOMOGRAPHY (pQCT)

What is it?
Peripheral quantitative computed tomography is a
special-purpose version of QCT that evaluates bone density in the wrist and forearm. It employs a dedicated CT
scanner that is specifically set up to measure bone mineral density.

How does it work?
During the procedure, you sit comfortably next to the
device. It has a doughnut hole–like opening, through
which you place your arm. Some devices are designed
for measuring the hip and leg. Scan time is generally
less than ten minutes.

As with quantitative CT used for spine measurements, pQCT produces a three-dimensional image and
provides a volumetric measurement.

How accurate is it?
In some studies, pQCT has been able to distinguish between patients with osteoporosis and patients without the
disease. The technology is also useful for monitoring
volunteers in clinical studies.

By comparison, pQCT is less sensitive than measurements using DXA. However, it correlates well with measurements obtained from ultrasound, another method of
measuring bone density.

How much does the test cost?
Costs vary; check with your physician.

p-DEXA

What is it?

The p-DEXA is a tabletop scanner that uses dual-energy X-ray absorptiometry to access bone density in the forearm. Clinical research suggests that bone density in the forearm reflects bone mineral density in the hip and spine.

What's more, the p-DEXA test is useful for monitoring the results of hormone replacement therapy (HRT), or other anti-osteoporosis drugs.

The *p* stands for *peripheral* or for *portable* (because the equipment can be carried to health fairs, pharmacies, and other sites).

How does it work?

Measuring the forearm takes approximately six to ten minutes, and your results are reported as a T-score. Exposure to radiation is low—less than you would receive during an average day outdoors. P-DEXA is a good alternative to DXA if you have a disability that makes it difficult to move onto a DXA table.

How accurate is it?

Because it uses dual-energy X-ray absorptiometry, p-DEXA is highly accurate, and thus a good option if DXA is not available. The p-DEXA does not diagnose osteoporosis but is used as an initial screening tool. It can be used to predict your chances of breaking a bone from osteoporosis. If the results indicate loss of bone density, your doctor will likely order a DXA scan as a follow-up.

How much does the test cost?
The test costs approximately $25.

PERIPHERAL INSTANTANEOUS X-RAY IMAGER BONE DENSITOMETER (PIXI)

What is it?
Made by Lunar, the PIXI is a small densitometer that uses dual-energy X-ray absorptiometry to measure bone density in the heel, a site that has been shown to correlate well to the hip and spine. For assessing the risk of osteoporosis, some medical experts prefer the heel over the forearm, because, like the hip, the heel is a weight-bearing site.

The PIXI is a screening test. It can also help monitor the effectiveness of anti-osteoporosis medicine.

The PIXI is widely used at health fairs, gyms, and clinics. It can also measure bone density in the forearm.

How does it work?
For a heel measurement, you place your foot inside the unit, and there is no need to remove your socks or panty hose. The PIXI is considered the world's fastest peripheral densitometer, with a scan time of approximately five seconds. Your results are reported as a T-score.

How accurate is it?
Because the PIXI uses DXA technology, it is considered accurate for the site it measures.

How much does the test cost?
The PIXI test usually costs $25.

accuDEXA (OF THE MIDDLE FINGER)

What is it?

accuDEXA is a tabletop unit developed by Schnick Technologies. It uses dual-energy X-ray absorptiometry (DXA) to evaluate bone mineral density in the middle portion of your third finger, a measurement site that has been used to assess bone mineral density for more than twenty years. Studies have shown that the finger is a good predictor, and that loss of bone density in the finger correlates with loss of bone density in the hip and spine. In other words, if you've lost density in your finger, you may have lost it in your hip or spine too.

How does it work?

accuDEXA is a low-level radiation test that can be performed in your doctor's office. In fact, radiation exposure is 1/150,000 of a chest X ray.

You simply place your hand over an ultrasensitive sensor inside the accuDEXA unit, and the scan takes less than two minutes. A touch pad automatically displays all pertinent data, and results are printed out. Like a DXA scan, your results are computed as a T-score and a Z-score.

How accurate is it?

The test is accurate for measuring bone density in the fingers.

How much does the test cost?

Costs vary and may range from $35 to $75 a test.

RADIOGRAPHIC ABSORPTIOMETRY (RA)

What is it?

First described in 1939, radiographic absorptiometry (RA) is an old technique for measuring bone mass, but one that has been updated by improvements in X-ray and computer technology. It is a convenient and reliable method for measuring bone mineral density in the fingers. Other advantages include:

- Ability to predict fracture risk

- Wide availability in many communities

- No radiation exposure to the torso

- Low radiation exposure

- Good precision

How does it work?

Prior to the procedure, you must remove any rings, although there is no need to disrobe. Next, you'll position your left hand on special film, and a small aluminum wedge is placed next to one of your fingers. This wedge serves as a comparative reference for a computerized analysis of the optical density of the bone. With a digital camera, an X-ray image of your hand—a picture called a radiograph—is produced on the film. For quality control purposes, the process is repeated at a different exposure.

Two exposed radiographs are sent to a testing laboratory for analysis. The images are captured electronically in a special video camera and evaluated to determine the average density of the middle portions of the second, third, and fourth fingers. Results from the two images are compared. If found to be in agreement (less than 3 percent difference), results are averaged. If not in agreement, the X-ray may have to be repeated.

Results are usually available in forty-eight hours and sent to the referring physician. Some units, however, can process the data on-site. This information can be used by a doctor to diagnose osteoporosis and recommend treatment strategies.

Bone mineral density from RA is reported in a measurement called arbitrary units, which reflect the degree of bone density in the fingers.

How accurate is it?

RA holds promise as a practical screening tool for osteoporosis and for predicting the risk of fracture. In a recent study, investigators compared the results of RA with those of DXA in a group of 389 postmenopausal women, aged 55 to 84. RA performed favorably to DXA.

The investigators concluded: "RA may therefore help to evaluate fracture risk, especially if no DXA is available." Other research has determined that the results of RA correlate well with QCT.

Another experiment found that RA could predict low bone density of the spine with a 90 percent degree of accuracy, and that of the hip with an 82 percent degree of accuracy. This finding led the researchers to state that "radiographic absorptiometry may be useful as a screening technique for primary care physicians and in research settings where dual-photon or dual-energy X-ray absorptiometry are impossible."

How much does the test cost?

Costs of this test can range from $60 to $120.

ULTRASOUND OF THE HEEL

What is it?

Available in doctors' offices, ultrasound of the heel uses high-frequency sound waves passed through bone and adjacent tissue to estimate bone mineral density and predict fracture risk. Ultrasound of the heel uses no radiation.

How does it work?

While seated comfortably, you slip your foot into a device that resembles a home foot massager. Most devices can perform the procedure in less than a minute. Results are expressed as a T-score.

How accurate is it?

There is disagreement among experts as to the accuracy of ultrasound of the heel. Some rate it as accurate; others say it's less precise than other methods of bone mineral testing. Accuracy ratings have not yet been established.

However, at least one study says that ultrasound of the heel can predict the risk of hip fracture in elderly women as well as DXA measurements of femoral bone mineral density. Researchers monitored 5,662 women (with an average age of 80) for hip fracture during a two-year period. At the start of the study, they obtained ultrasound measurements of the heel and DXA measurements of femoral bone mineral density.

After adjusting for age, the researchers found that low heel ultrasound measurements and a low femoral bone mineral density were similarly associated with an increased risk of fracture. They concluded that ultrasound of the heel can predict the risk of hip fracture as well as DXA. Other evidence indicates that ultrasound used in combination with DXA is a good predictor of fracture risk.

Even so, many medical experts feel that ultrasound of the heel doesn't correlate to having a DXA of the hip, but that it is still very useful as a screening tool. If an ultrasound of your heel reveals something is amiss, your doctor should order a DXA.

How much does the test cost?
In most places, ultrasound of the heel costs $35.

SHOULD YOU CONSIDER A PERIPHERAL TEST?

Peripheral tests are excellent screening tools for most age groups. However, when you enter an age or period in life that puts you at higher risk for osteoporosis, a peripheral test may not be your best choice. In a 1997 article published in *Calcified Tissue International*, a group of prominent bone specialists outlined testing strategies for various categories of women, based on age and risk factors for osteoporosis and fractures. Below are their recommendations for using peripheral and central bone density measurements.

You're younger than age 65 and/or you're within fifteen years of menopause.

PREFERRED STRATEGY: A bone density test of your spine by DXA or QCT, since the risk of spinal fractures is high in this category. Also, a DXA of the hip to establish a baseline for future measurements, as well to gauge any loss of density.

ACCEPTABLE STRATEGY: A spinal bone density test only, measured by DXA or QCT.

ALTERNATIVE STRATEGY: Peripheral measurements taken by SXA, RA, p-DEXA, or ultrasound.

You're 65 or older, and it has been more than fifteen years since menopause.

PREFERRED STRATEGY: After age 65, you're at a much higher risk for a hip fracture. Accordingly, have a bone density test of the hip by DXA, and the spine by either QCT or lateral DXA. QCT and lateral DXA tests can better detect the presence of degenerative spinal abnormalities, which are common in this age group.

ACCEPTABLE STRATEGY: A DXA of your hip only.

ALTERNATIVE STRATEGY: Past age 65, bone is lost equally from all skeletal sites. Therefore, peripheral tests can provide valuable information. In fact, they are more useful in this age group than for women younger than 65. A good alternative strategy is to have peripheral measurements taken by SXA, RA, p-DEXA, or ultrasound.

NOT RECOMMENDED: A bone density test of your spine only. As noted above, spinal tests in this age group reveal skeletal abnormalities, which can skew the results of bone density tests.

You've been diagnosed with osteoporosis and are undergoing therapy.

PREFERRED STRATEGY: Your physician should monitor your response to drug therapy by ordering a bone density test at regular intervals. The best tests for monitoring therapy are spinal measurements by DXA or QCT, and hip measurements by DXA. If the anti-osteoporosis drug is working as it should, your spine will show bone density increases of several percent the first year. (Another effective way to monitor the effectiveness of therapy is through a biochemical bone marker test, discussed below.)

ACCEPTABLE STRATEGY: A DXA or QCT of the spine. The spine is the bodily site most responsive to therapy.

NOT RECOMMENDED: A peripheral bone density test, particularly if you're taking anti-osteoporosis medicine and need to know if the drug is working. Although precise, peripheral tests do not do a good job of monitoring response to therapy.

Biochemical Bone Marker Testing

What is it?
Biochemical bone marker testing involves a simple urine test that lets your doctor easily and conveniently measure your rate of bone resorption (the process of bone tissue removal) and bone formation.

As osteoclasts degrade bone, they release a variety of by-products ("markers") of bone breakdown into the bloodstream. These by-products, which include hydroxyproline and pyridinoline, eventually are excreted in the urine.

Similarly, as osteoblasts form new bone protein, they release markers such as osteocalcin into circulation. Bone formation markers are also excreted in the urine.

How does it work?

A urine sample is taken in the morning and sent to a laboratory for analysis. The results indicate whether your rate of bone resorption is normal or too high. A high level of bone resorption markers, for example, may indicate that your body is breaking down bone faster than it can be replaced—an imbalance that can lead to bone loss. If the test shows a high rate of resorption, your doctor may order a bone mineral density test, such as a DXA scan. Newer tests have been developed that measure bone markers in serum, the watery portion of blood.

Who should be tested?

You are a candidate for the test if you:

- Are past menopause.

- Are taking anti-osteoporosis medicine.

- Have a family history of osteoporosis.

- Are thin, or small-boned.

- Have been diagnosed with a bone disease.

- Don't get much exercise.

- Don't consume enough calcium in your diet.

- Smoke, or drink alcohol excessively.

- Consume excessive caffeine.

- Are taking certain drugs known to cause bone loss.

TABLE 6.1
Major bone density tests now in use

Test	Measurement Sites	Advantages	Disadvantages	Cost
Dual-energy X-ray absorptiometry (DXA)	Total body, spine, hip, or forearm	• Multiple measurement sites • Can distinguish between bone and soft tissue • Low radiation exposure • High accuracy	• Not portable • Not universally available	$150–$300
Single-energy X-ray absorptiometry (SXA)	Heel or forearm	• Low radiation exposure • Quick	• Can measure just two sites	$50–$150
Quantitative computed tomography (QCT)	Lumbar spine, peripheral parts of the skeleton	• Can distinguish between cortical and trabecular bone • Can measure true volumetric density of bone	• High radiation dose • Not entirely reproducible • More expensive than other tests	$150–$400

TABLE 6.1—Continued

Test	Measurement Sites	Advantages	Disadvantages	Cost
Peripheral quantitative CT (pQCT)	Wrist and forearm	• Useful for monitoring patients in clinical studies • Portable	• Used only for measuring peripheral sites • Less sensitive than DXA	Varies
p-DEXA	Forearm	• A good screening tool • Quick	• Used only for measuring a peripheral site • Not a diagnostic tool	$25
PIXI	Heel	• A good screening tool • Very quick • Portable	• Used only for measuring a peripheral site • Not a diagnostic tool	$25
accuDEXA	Fingers	• Low radiation exposure • Quick • Correlates with loss of bone density in the hip and spine	• Used only for measuring a peripheral site • Not a diagnostic tool	$35–$75

TABLE 6.1—Continued

Test	Measurement Sites	Advantages	Disadvantages	Cost
Radiographic absorptiometry (RA)	Fingers	• Can be performed using conventional X-ray equipment • Low radiation exposure • No radiation exposure to torso • Wide availability	• Measures only one site • Films must be sent to a processing lab	$60–$120
Ultrasound	Heel	• Radiation free • A good screening tool • Portable	• Measures only one site • Not possible to measure potential fracture sites such as the hip or spine	$35

Adapted from: Kleerekoper, M. 1998. Detecting osteoporosis. *Postgraduate Medicine* 103:45–47; and Woodhead, G. A., et al. 1998. Osteoporosis: diagnosis and prevention. *Nurse Practitioner* 23:18, 23–27.

How accurate is it?

By giving a bone marker test, your doctor can evaluate whether osteoporosis-fighting drugs are doing their job; adjust dosages, if necessary; and weigh the consequences of discontinuing treatment. Suppose you're taking 0.3 milligrams of estrogen as part of therapy. With this test, your doctor can check to see if that's enough to keep your bone markers where they should be. The test thus complements, monitors, and evaluates osteoporosis treatment. In addition, research shows that bone marker tests may be useful in predicting the risk of fracture.

A bone marker test, however, does not substitute for a bone density test such as a DXA scan. Further, bone marker tests are not universally considered to be good screening tools because they are not as sensitive as bone density tests.

How much does the test cost?

A bone marker urine test costs about $50, depending on the laboratory. The test is reimbursable by Medicare in most states.

Emerging Technologies: Magnetic Resonance Imaging (MRI)

Newer technologies to measure bone density are under development, while existing technologies are being refined and adapted to assess bone density. One of these is magnetic resonance imaging (MRI).

Through the use of powerful magnetism, radio waves, and computer technology, MRI produces detailed pictures of internal parts of the body. These pictures are transferred to film, enhanced by sophisticated computer technology, and evaluated by the physician to determine the diagnosis and treatment. MRIs are used to detect disease at its earliest stages, when treatment is most successful. No X rays are used, and MRI exams are safe, painless, and noninvasive.

It is vital to emphasize that MRI cannot be performed on patients with cardiac pacemakers, heart valve replacements, and other implantable devices.

Until recently, MRIs were used mostly for studying soft tissues. However, newly developed MRI techniques are being used to study trabecular bone, and early studies hint that MRI may be a promising tool for assessing osteoporosis.

7.

Based on My Results, What's Next?

Your bone-health needs are as unique as your personality. And those needs change with each stage in life. Add to your life-stage the results of a bone density test, and your needs become even more well defined. A plan geared toward meeting those needs is exactly what you need to strengthen your bones and feel your best, at any age.

A good first step is to give some thought to your test results (if you've had a bone density test), risk factors for osteoporosis, and your life-stage (perimenopause, menopause, or postmenopause).

Then look through the following profiles, and see where you fit in. Once you've identified your niche, discuss with your physician the prevention/treatment strategies described below. These strategies are based on the *Guidelines of Care on Osteoporosis for the Primary Care Physician,* published in 1998 by the Foundation for Osteoporosis Research and Education (FORE), as well as on available medical literature and research on osteoporosis treatments.

YOU'RE PREMENOPAUSAL

If you're in your thirties or mid to late forties, some doctors may refer to you as "premenopausal." This stage of life generally describes a period prior to menopause. During premenopause, there are not yet any classic menopausal symptoms, such as hot flashes or vaginal dryness.

Granted, you may not think much about osteoporosis or any other disease, for that matter, during this time. Still, you must take preventive measures such as getting enough calcium. Make sure you consume at least 1,000 milligrams daily so that you enter menopause with as much mineral in your bones as possible. This should be easy to do with a calcium-rich diet. You'll need to supplement if you can't drink milk or eat diary products.

Another excellent defense is to exercise to build up your bone density before age-related losses take their toll later. In a study at the University of California in San Francisco, sixty-three women ranging in age from 20 to 35 were randomly assigned to exercising and nonexercising groups. The exercisers did aerobics and weight training for one hour three times a week. All the women received calcium supplements or a placebo.

After two years, the exercisers had shored up their bone density in the spine, hips, and heels. The obvious lesson is that you can build bone early on with regular exercise and adequate calcium intake.

The lesson here: Get moving now to keep your bones strong later!

If you've had a bone density test that reveals osteopenia (low bone mass), your doctor may prescribe birth control pills. Research shows that oral contraceptives produce a modest increase in bone density in the spine and may be protective in other sites as well.

YOU'RE IN PERIMENOPAUSE, WITH NO MAJOR RISK FACTORS

Perimenopause ("around" menopause) is a period of fluctuating estrogen levels that hits about two years prior to menopause and continues for the next two years following menopause. This four-year period generally occurs sometime between the ages of 35 and 50. Symptoms of perimenopause are similar to those of premenstrual syndrome (PMS): bloating, weight gain, depression, headaches, food cravings, and lack of energy.

If you have no major risk factors for osteoporosis, your best bet now is to follow—and maintain—a bone-smart lifestyle. Strategies are outlined on pages 102–103. (Note: "Major" risk factors include fracture history, family history of osteoporosis, bone-depleting disease or medicines, interrupted menstrual history, hysterectomy prior to menopause, or immobility for six months or longer.)

YOU'RE IN PERIMENOPAUSE, WITH ONE OR MORE RISK FACTORS FOR OSTEOPOROSIS

At this point in your life, you probably need a bone mineral density test if you:

- Have been on corticosteroids or anticonvulsive medication for a long time.

- Suffer from any disease that can result in bone loss.

- Have lost your period for six months or longer (with the exception of pregnancy).

- Had a hysterectomy prior to menopause.

- Have poor calcium intake.

- Engage in habits, such as smoking or alcohol abuse, that increase your risk.

- Have had restricted mobility for six months or longer.

- Have a family history of osteoporosis.

- Have had a "nonviolent" fracture (i.e., you've already broken a bone as an adult, falling from a standing position, as opposed to fracturing a bone in an automobile accident).

Depending on your test results, your physician may recommend various measures to slow the progression of bone loss. For example:

If your T-score is −1 or better:
- Follow the bone-smart recommendations listed on pages 103–104.

- Increase your calcium intake to 1,500 milligrams a day (from food and supplements), in counsel with your physician.

- Plan to have another bone density test in two to five years, or at menopause.

If your T-score is between −1 and −2:
- Follow the bone-smart recommendations listed on pages 103–104.

- Take 1,500 milligrams of calcium a day (from food and supplements), as recommended by your physician.

- Discuss the possible need for vitamin D supplementation with your physician.

- Engage in a regular program of weight-bearing exercise.

- Talk to your physician about evaluating you for secondary causes of bone loss.

- Consider estrogen/oral contraceptive therapy.

- Your physician may order a bone marker test if rapid bone loss is suspected. In cases of rapid bone loss, an anti-osteoporosis drug may be prescribed.

- Plan to repeat the bone density test in two years, or at menopause.

If your T-score is −2 or worse:
- Follow the bone-smart recommendations listed on pages 103–104.

- Take 1,500 milligrams of calcium a day (from food and supplements), as recommended by your physician.

- Talk to your physician about evaluating you for secondary causes of bone loss.

- Consider treatment with oral contraceptives, HRT, or other anti-osteoporosis medication.

- Have another bone density test in one to two years.

YOU'RE IN MENOPAUSE

Menopause comes naturally to most women at midlife, usually between ages 45 and 55. Medically, it refers to your final menstrual period. Your ovaries stop functioning, and they produce fewer hormones. Signs of impending menopause include irregular periods, six months without a period, or hot flashes. Your physician can confirm that you are close to menopause with a blood test that measures follicle-stimulating hormone (FSH). Bone loss accelerates at menopause, so it's vital that you have a bone density test now if you haven't already.

If your bone density is normal, the best course of action is to continue following a bone-smart lifestyle. To keep your bones from a downhill slope, eat a calcium-rich diet and regularly engage in a program of regular weight-bearing exercise.

This period is also the time in your life to start eating more soy foods. Soy foods contain health-building chemicals called phytoestrogens that can help normalize estrogen levels. Menopausal women typically have low levels of estrogens, and these can be raised by phytoestrogens. Add a serving of soy to your daily diet—one that provides about 30 to 50 milligrams of isoflavones. That's roughly the amount found in one-half cup of tofu, a cup of soy milk, or a handful of soy nuts.

If your bone density is low, you may have to take further steps in addition to following a bone-smart lifestyle. Your physician, for example, may initiate drug therapy to reduce your fracture risk or prevent osteoporosis if:

- Your T-score shows osteopenia, and you have no known risk factors for osteoporosis.

- You have risk factors, and your T-score indicates osteopenia.

- You have been diagnosed with osteoporosis. (A T-score of −2.5 or worse is considered a diagnosis of osteoporosis.)

Therapy may include hormone replacement therapy (HRT) if:

- You have menopausal symptoms.

- Your ovaries were removed before age 50.

- You experienced natural menopause before age 50.

- You have multiple risk factors for osteoporosis.

HRT has proven to be the best treatment to stop the bone loss of menopause. However, the decision to go on HRT requires careful thought because of its potential side effects. If you're at risk of breast cancer, for example, a better choice may be raloxifene (Evista). Other alternatives to HRT include alendronate (Fosamax), calcitonin, or a natural medicine called ipriflavone. These are discussed in chapter 10.

In addition, have follow-up bone density tests at regular intervals, as recommended by your physician. Follow the bone-smart recommendations listed in table 7.1, including increased calcium intake.

YOU'RE POSTMENOPAUSAL

Postmenopause is a naturally occurring stage of life in which you have been free of menstrual periods for at least one year. If you've never had a bone density test,

be sure to have one now. Bone loss accelerates at two
points in your life—around menopause and again at age
65—so it's essential that you take the proper therapeutic
measures. It's never too late to halt bone loss and decrease your risk of fracture.

If your T-score is −1 or better:
  ▪ Follow a bone-smart lifestyle, which may include
increasing calcium intake to 1,500 milligrams daily
(from food or supplements).

  ▪ Consider HRT as a way to prevent osteoporosis,
but weigh advantages and disadvantages first. Discuss
HRT with your physician.

  ▪ Consider alendronate (Fosamax) or raloxifene (Evista) as an alternative to HRT to prevent osteoporosis.
Discuss these alternatives with your physician.

  ▪ Investigate natural-medicine treatments such as
ipriflavone.

  ▪ Have another bone density test in one to three
years, or as recommended by your physician.

If your T-score is between −1 and −2:
  ▪ Adopt a bone-smart lifestyle, which may include
increasing calcium intake to 1,500 milligrams daily
(from food or supplements).

  ▪ With three to four risk factors, consider anti-
osteoporosis medication; with five risk factors, your
physician may initiate treatment.

■ Have another bone density test in one to two years, or as recommended by your physician, to monitor the effectiveness of treatment.

If your T-score is −2 or worse:

■ Adopt a bone-smart lifestyle, which may include increasing calcium intake to 1,500 milligrams daily (from food or supplements).

■ Talk to your physician about upping your intake of vitamin D to 800 a day (from food and supplements), particularly if more than ten years have elapsed since menopause.

■ Your physician may prescribe alendronate (Fosamax), HRT, or raloxifene (Evista). If it has been five years or more since you experienced menopause, your physician may prescribe calcitonin.

■ Exercise on a regular basis. In areas where your bones are the weakest, your physician may suggest special exercises that target those points.

It's never too late to begin exercising, either. Even in people [women] over age 50, exercise can help restore up to 5 percent of bone loss. In 1994, the results of a landmark study of postmenopausal women were published, showing for the first time that a single treatment—weight training—reduced risk factors for spine and hip fractures, which accompany osteoporosis. At the USDA Human Nutrition Research Center on Aging at Tufts University, women aged 50 to 70 worked out on exercise machines twice a week for a year. At the end of the study, they had built up their bones, increased their strength and muscle mass, and improved their balance.

▪ If you're taking medication such as HRT or alendronate (Fosamax), your physician may monitor their effectiveness with bone marker tests. In addition, have follow-up bone density tests at regular intervals (usually one to two years), as recommended by your physician.

TABLE 7.1
Bone-Smart Lifestyle Strategies
----

1. Consume enough calcium each day. To maximize and preserve bone loss, you should take in at least 1,000 milligrams of calcium a day (from food and supplements) if you're in the age group 19–50 and 1,200 milligrams if you're 51 or older. Many physicians recommend 1,500 milligrams daily, particularly if risk factors for osteoporosis are involved. (See chapter 8 for more information on calcium.)

2. Consume an adequate amount of vitamin D each day. This means 400 IU of vitamin D daily. Taking vitamin D helps your body absorb calcium.

3. Engage in weight-bearing exercise. Weight-bearing and strength-developing exercise stimulates the formation of bone. It also improves strength and balance, thus reducing the risk of falls and fractures.

Weight-bearing exercise involves activity in which your bones and muscles work against gravity as your feet and legs bear your body weight. Examples include walking, jogging, stair climbing, dancing, and tennis. Strength-developing exercise is essentially strength training (weight lifting), which builds body-firming muscle and bone strength.

4. Avoid tobacco use. Smoking is the single largest preventable cause of premature death and disability. Further, it damages your skeletal structure and is a serious risk factor for osteoporosis. If you're a smoker, make a conscientious effort to quit. While there is no single tried-and-true method for quitting smoking, the decision to quit generally begins with a commitment on your part. Smoking cessation programs can be quite effective. Other supportive aids such as nicotine gum and a change in routine may help too.

5. Keep alcohol intake moderate. Alcohol abuse is detrimental to bone health, as well. Further, it can lead to falls and accidents, as well as social, psychological, and emotional problems. If you drink alcohol, do so in moderation.

YOU'RE POSTMENOPAUSAL, WITH SEVERE OSTEOPOROSIS

If you've been diagnosed with severe osteoporosis (usually a T-score of −2.5 or worse), your physician may prescribe a combined therapy such as HRT plus alendronate (Fosamax), or HRT plus calcitriol. Alendronate does an excellent job of improving bone mass in seniors. The natural medicine ipriflavone also appears to stimulate new bone growth and decrease fracture rate among seniors.

In addition to taking bone-saving medication, continue to follow a lifestyle that includes a calcium and vitamin D-rich diet, plus regular sessions of weight-bearing and strength-developing exercise. Refrain from body-jolting exercises such as high-impact aerobics that could increase your risk of fracture.

If you're taking medication for osteoporosis, your physician may monitor their effectiveness with bone marker tests. In addition, have follow-up bone density tests at regular intervals, as recommended by your physician.

Also important: Approximately 30 percent of all people over the age of 60 will fall each year. Work with your physician to evaluate your risk of falling. Then make some changes around your home to help you prevent falls and thus reduce your risk of fracture. For example:

- Increase the lighting around your home.

- Use night lights.

- Limit glare.

- Reduce clutter.

- Create more walking space.

- Avoid waxed or wet floors.

- Repair frayed carpet.

- Raise the height of your toilet seats.

- Apply special appliques to tile floors or bathtubs for a better grip underfoot.

- Install hand rails.

- Repair any broken steps.

- Use chairs with arms.

8.

Which Nutrients Build Bone Density?

Without question, nutrition is now widely accepted as part of a strategy to improve bone density and bone health. There are many nutrients that can help you build and maintain the density of your bones.

This chapter delves into the key nutrients that enhance bone density; the next chapter shows you how to incorporate them, along with specific foods, into a bone-healthy diet.

CALCIUM

What does calcium do?

Of all minerals in your body, calcium is the most abundant. It accounts for 40 percent of your skeleton, and about 99 percent of the calcium in your body is deposited in bones and teeth. These structures are hardened and strengthened by calcium, working in combination with the mineral phosphorus. The remaining 1 percent of the body's calcium is concentrated in the soft tissues, where it plays an essential role in muscle contraction, nerve transmission, blood coagulation, and the activity of the heart.

No matter what your age, you need an ongoing supply of calcium flowing in and out of your bones to maintain bone strength and bone health. Dietary calcium has a positive effect on your body even if you already have osteoporosis. Case in point: In a study of fourteen postmenopausal women with osteoporosis, calcium supplements (1,000 milligrams daily for eight days) significantly reduced bone resorption—the breakdown of bone.

Although calcium is vital for bone health, it is being researched for other health benefits. For example, new studies suggest that it may help regulate your blood pressure, improve symptoms of premenstrual tension, and reduce your risk of colon cancer.

What foods are high in calcium?

Dairy products are the best known of the calcium-rich foods, with a cup of skim milk supplying about 290 milligrams. Vegetables are high in calcium as well, and some of the best sources are kale, and turnip greens, and broccoli. Another excellent source is canned salmon with bones.

Unfortunately, our bodies don't absorb all the calcium we eat from foods. In fact, only about 20 to 30 percent is actually taken in. What's more, we absorb less as we age.

To make matters worse, certain foods and substances can interfere with the absorption and use of calcium. Whole grains are one example. The fiber in these foods tends to bind with calcium and carry it out of the body, causing depletion. Phytates (phosphorus groups) in fiber also block calcium absorption. The same is true of oxalic acid, a substance found in spinach, beet greens, and chard.

On the other hand, certain factors can improve the absorption of calcium, especially the presence of vitamins A, C, and D. Vitamin D, in particular, helps calcium penetrate cell membranes so that it can nourish the body tissues where it's needed.

There's lots of data piling up too that adequate calcium intake and exercise early in life help ward off bone loss later in life. A study of younger women, 25 to 34 years old, showed that a combination of regular exercise (running and walking) and high calcium intake—either by diet or supplementation—can build bone mass in the spine by up to 15 percent. The results suggest that the combination of calcium and exercise may protect against osteoporosis in later years.

Getting your fill of calcium each day is not difficult, as table 8.1 shows.

How can I boost my calcium intake?
Here's a strategy to get the most calcium from your diet and keep your bones healthy:

- Eat a varied, well-balanced diet containing enough calories to meet your energy needs.

- Include two to three servings of low-fat dairy products every day, including those fortified with vitamin D.

- If you supplement, take your calcium supplement with a meal to maximize absorption.

TABLE 8.1
A Healthy Day's Worth of Calcium

Food	Measure	Calcium (mg)
Orange juice, calcium-fortified	1 cup	300
Skim milk	1 cup	302
Tofu	4 ounces	108
Low-fat yogurt	8 ounces	415
Turnip greens, cooked, chopped	1 cup	249
Total		*1,374 mg*

Adapted from: Brown, J. 1990. The science of human nutrition.
New York: Harcourt Brace Jovanovich. 315–316.

- Avoid consuming caffeine and very high fiber foods at the same meal with high-calcium foods. Both can prevent calcium from doing its job.

- Maintain a regular exercise program. Inactivity is an enemy of calcium. Your body uses this essential mineral better when you're active.

- Don't smoke. Smoking interferes with the body's ability to metabolize and use calcium.

- Keep alcohol consumption to a minimum. Alcohol decreases calcium absorption and increases calcium losses.

Should I supplement with calcium?

For women, the recommended daily intake for calcium from food and supplements is 1,000 milligrams (ages 19–50) and 1,200 milligrams (51 and older). Many medical experts recommend 1,500 milligrams daily after menopause. Check with your doctor.

Most women concerned about osteoporosis want to

know if they should take calcium supplements to bridge nutritional gaps. The answer is—yes.

Many women do not eat nutritiously enough even to satisfy the Recommended Dietary Allowances (RDA) for calcium, according to research. And with age, your need for calcium and other nutrients changes. If you're older than 60, for example, your body has trouble absorbing enough calcium and so you must take in an additional supply.

Which calcium supplements are best?

If you supplement, calcium carbonate and calcium citrate are good choices because they contain among the highest percentages of calcium. Make sure you stick to brands from well-known manufacturers.

If you hate to swallow pills, try a chewable antacid such as Tums, formulated with calcium carbonate. Avoid antacids that contain aluminum, however. They can pull calcium from your bones and cause your body to excrete it. (Tums is aluminum-free.)

Another option is to supplement with soft-chew forms of calcium. One example is Mead Johnson Nutritionals' Viactiv, formulated with a combination of vitamin D and vitamin K, along with calcium. Antacids and many other calcium supplements do not contain these additional nutrients, which are vital to bone health.

Viactiv comes in three flavors—milk chocolate, "mochacinno," and caramel—and was the first calcium supplement of this type on the market. Another soft-chew product is CalBurst from Nature's Way.

You can get your daily dose of calcium from calcium-fortified foods too, such as fruit juice, spritzers, and other specialty products.

MAGNESIUM

What does magnesium do?

Magnesium is in charge of more than four-hundred metabolic reactions in your body. In small amounts, it is vital for bone health. Magnesium is essential for getting calcium out of the bloodstream and into your bones. It helps your body absorb vitamin D, a bone-protective nutrient involved in the absorption of calcium. Research into magnesium and osteoporosis indicates that:

- Postmenopausal women with osteoporosis tend to be magnesium-needy, suggesting that magnesium is an important factor in building bone density.

- Magnesium supplements given to menopausal women over a two-year period prevented fractures and significantly increased bone density.

- Magnesium supplementation helps suppress the cycle that leads to bone breakdown.

What foods are high in magnesium?

You can usually obtain the recommended daily amount of magnesium (280 milligrams daily for women) from a healthy, well-balanced diet. Magnesium-rich foods include chickpeas, beet greens, turnip greens, fruits, and whole grains. A study in the *American Journal of Clinical Nutrition* found that lifelong intake of fruits and vegetables—good sources of magnesium—helps prevent the loss of bone density.

Should I supplement with magnesium?

It's best to get your magnesium from food. However, an all-around vitamin-mineral supplement taken daily will help protect against deficiencies. Most products contain about 100 milligrams of magnesium.

BORON

What does boron do?
Boron is trace mineral that has great importance in nutrition, especially in mineral metabolism. It helps your body properly use other minerals, guards against calcium losses, converts vitamin D into its active form, and thus may be a factor in preventing osteoporosis.

In a study of postmenopausal women, for example, boron supplementation greatly reduced the amount of calcium and magnesium excretion and increased blood levels of a natural form of estrogen. (Essential for bone health, estrogen effectively slows the loss of calcium from bone in postmenopausal women.) The findings suggest that boron may be important in the prevention and treatment of osteoporosis. Boron also strengthens bones.

What foods are high in boron?
Boron is found in tomatoes, green peppers, and other vegetables.

Should I supplement with boron?
Although there is no Recommended Dietary Allowance for boron, recent studies with postmenopausal women suggest that supplementation may be advisable. Multivitamin-mineral supplements contain about 150 micrograms.

COPPER

What does copper do?

Found in all body tissues, copper is a busy mineral. It assists in bone and collagen formation, energy metabolism, nerve transmission, and red cell production. Most of the copper in your body is stored in your liver. However, significant amounts are found in the skin, brain, bone marrow, bone, and muscle too.

Copper influences bone health by governing the action of an enzyme involved in the construction of collagen. If copper is deficient, collagen construction is faulty—a problem than can manifest itself in osteoporosis, among other health problems.

High levels of fructose in your diet can keep the body from properly using copper. Fructose is a simple sugar found in fruit, fruit juices, and high-fructose corn syrup, which is a common sweetener. In studies of postmenopausal women, eating too much fructose promoted bone loss, particularly when the subjects' diets were low in copper.

What foods are high in copper?

Copper is present in nutritionally significant amounts in nearly all foods. It is particularly abundant in shellfish, liver, cherries, whole grains, eggs, poultry, and beans.

Should I supplement with copper?

For good health, you need between 1.5 to 3 milligrams a day of copper. By eating a well-balanced diet with a variety of wholesome foods, you should take in plenty of copper. Multivitamin-mineral supplements generally contain 2 milligrams of copper.

MANGANESE

What does manganese do?
One of the trace minerals, manganese is involved in the formation of bone and cartilage. It also plays a role in protein, carbohydrate, and fat production.

Deficiency symptoms include poor muscular coordination, abnormal brain function, glucose tolerance problems, and poor skeletal and cartilage formation. One cause of manganese deficiency appears to be the consumption of simple sugars. In one study of men and women, sugar was substituted for complex carbohydrates in a diet that provided ample dietary manganese. This substitution, however, caused manganese levels to drop.

Low levels of manganese have been linked to osteoporosis. In one study, concentrations of manganese in osteoporotic women were found to be just 25 percent of normal women. This suggests that adequate manganese may be important in the prevention of osteoporosis.

What foods are high in manganese?
Whole grain cereals, egg yolks, and green vegetables are among the richest food sources of manganese.

Should I supplement with manganese?
A balanced diet provides roughly 4 milligrams of manganese a day, well within recommended levels for adults. That being so, there's no need to supplement with extra manganese. Multivitamin-mineral supplements contain around 2 milligrams for extra insurance against a shortfall.

FLUORIDE

What does fluoride do?

This essential trace mineral is a guardian angel of sorts, protecting you against tooth decay throughout life, and may help treat osteoporosis. When taken in proper doses, fluoride encourages the *mineralization* of the forming primary and permanent teeth. Mineralization occurs in the tooth enamel, a crystalline structure whose major component is the hydroxyl molecule, and results in teeth that are stronger and more resistant to decay.

Fluoride also prevents a process called *demineralization,* which weakens the tooth enamel. It occurs when bacterial plaque and carbohydrates form acids that dissolve into the enamel, creating microscopic subsurface lesions. Without adequate fluoride, the dissolving enamel will be whisked away by saliva. As this progressive demineralization continues, the tooth surface eventually collapses. The result is the formation of a detectable cavity.

But when fluoride is present in the saliva on a consistent basis, it adheres to the tooth enamel crystals and reduces the lesion size by making the crystals larger and more resistant to acid deterioration. This process is called *remineralization.* Fluoride also protects the root surfaces of teeth, making them more resistant to decay.

Fluoride supplementation has long been studied as a possible therapy for osteoporosis because it stimulates the formation of new bone cells. In a study published in 1995, treatment with fluoride (25 milligrams daily), plus calcium citrate (400 milligrams twice a day), was shown to strengthen bones and prevent vertebral fractures in women with osteoporosis. In many countries, fluoride therapy for osteoporosis is common, but its approval for use in the United States is pending. (For additional information on fluoride as a drug, see chapter 10.)

What foods are high in fluoride?
Fluoride is found in fluoridated water supplies; children's fluoride supplements; toothpastes, mouth rinses, and gels; beverages such as brewed tea, beer, and grape juice; and foods such as poultry, seafood, and spinach.

Should I supplement with fluoride?
Fluoride supplements are prescribed mostly for children who live in nonfluoridated areas.

The recommended daily amount of fluoride from all sources (water, food, and dental products) is expressed as adequate intake (AI)—the level required to reduce cavities without causing fluorosis. The AI of fluoride is 0.05 milligrams per kilogram (2.2 pounds) of body weight a day.

As a practical example, let's say you weigh 150 pounds (68 kilograms). A daily intake of 3.4 milligrams would thus provide protection against tooth decay. This was calculated by multiplying 0.05 milligrams by 68 kilograms.

The amount of fluoride consumed from optimally fluoridated water averages about 1 to 2 milligrams a day, with another 0.2 to 0.6 milligrams coming from food and other sources. Although we take in fluoride from numerous sources, it is worth mentioning that part of the ingested fluoride is retained in our teeth and bones, but much is excreted.

Excess fluoride can be toxic. Daily intakes of 20 to 80 milligrams or more for years can lead to serious toxicity symptoms, which include nausea, vomiting, diarrhea, and abdominal pain. These are often accompanied by seizures, heart arrhythmias, and coma. Fluoride can cause death at one-time megadosages of 5 to 10 grams. That's more than 10,000 to 20,000 times as much fluoride as is consumed in an eight-ounce glass of fluoridated water.

SILICON

What does silicon do?
A trace mineral found in plants, silicon is necessary for the formation of collagen in bones and connective tissue. In the early stages of bone growth, it aids in calcium absorption. One study found that silicon significantly increased bone density in the hip region of women with osteoporosis. This mineral is also essential for healthy nails, skin, and hair.

What foods are high in silicon?
Silicon-rich foods include alfalfa, beets, brown rice, bell peppers, soybeans, green leafy vegetables, and whole grains. Supplemental silicon is derived from extracts of the herb horsetail or from algae.

Should I supplement with silicon?
There's no recommended daily intake of silicon. A good diet provides all the silicon you need. Multivitamin-mineral supplements generally contain about 2 milligrams.

ZINC

What does zinc do?
Zinc has many roles in the body. For example, it helps absorb vitamins; break down carbohydrates; synthesize

nucleic acid, which directs the manufacture of protein in cells; and regulate the growth and development of reproductive organs.

Also, zinc is a trace mineral that appears to be a factor in preventing osteoporosis, especially when teamed up with other minerals. A study of postmenopausal women found that supplementing daily with 1,000 milligrams of calcium, 2.5 milligrams of copper, 5 milligrams of manganese, and 15 milligrams of zinc helped arrest bone loss in the lower spine.

What foods are high in zinc?
The best sources are lean proteins and whole grains.

Should I supplement with zinc?
Women need about 12 milligrams of zinc daily for good health. This amount is easily supplied by diet and by a multivitamin-mineral supplement.

VITAMIN D

What does vitamin D do?
This fat-soluble vitamin assists in the formation and maintenance of bones and teeth, is vital for a healthy nervous system, and helps protect the health of the heart.

Calcium simply can't be deposited into bones unless vitamin D is there to help. If vitamin D is in short supply, your bones will actually lose some of their calcium. The result is loss of bone strength and greater risk of fracture.

Vitamin D also helps maintain a normal ratio of calcium and phosphorus in the blood, plus it helps your body break down phosphorus.

Studies of the nutrient's bone-protective effects show

that supplementation with vitamin D (daily dosage, in international units, shown in parenthesis):

- Decreases wintertime bone loss (400 IU a day).

- Reduces the loss of bone density in postmenopausal women (100 IU or 700 IU a day).

- Boosts bone density in elderly women after two years of treatment (400 IU a day).

- Decreases significantly the occurrence of fractures when taken with calcium for eighteen months (800 IU of vitamin D and 1,200 milligrams of calcium a day).

What are the best sources of vitamin D?

You might be interested in learning that sunlight—rather than food—is the way we get most of our vitamin D. Sunlight activates a substance in the skin and turns it into vitamin D. All you need is about five to fifteen minutes of sunlight exposure two to three times a week. Unless you stay indoors all the time, you probably get enough from regular exposure to the sun.

Conveniently, many milk products, which are great sources of calcium, are routinely fortified with vitamin D. So if you drink milk, you're automatically getting a vitamin D supplement. A glass of milk contains about 100 IU of vitamin D.

Should I supplement with vitamin D?

Because the significance of vitamin D in bone health has been reemphasized, the recommended daily intake is 200 IU for women ages 19 through 50 years old. For the age group 51 through 70 years, the recommended daily intake has been upped to 400 IU. If you're 70 or older, you need 600 IU. Some physicians may recommend 800 IU daily.

If you're concerned about adequate vitamin D intake, consider supplementation. Multivitamin products contain around 400 IU, and calcium supplements such as Viactiv are formulated with 100 IU per chew.

The level of vitamin D considered too high is 2,000 IU daily over a long period of time. Ingesting this amount or more on a continual basis is extremely toxic. Continued overdosing can force calcium to be deposited in the heart, kidneys, and other soft tissues. Calcium deposits in the heart can cause death.

VITAMIN K

What does vitamin K do?

Admittedly, we don't hear much about vitamin K. But it is best known for its role in manufacturing proteins that help with normal clotting of the blood. However, research has revealed a side to vitamin K that most people have never seen: It is vital for building healthy bones, as well as for treating and preventing osteoporosis—which is why a number of calcium supplements are now being formulated with vitamin K.

Vitamin K comes in three forms: vitamin K_1, derived from plants; vitamin K_2, manufactured from bacteria in the intestine; and vitamin K_3, a synthetic form used to treat people who cannot utilize naturally occurring forms of vitamin K.

All three members of the trio are equally involved in the normal clotting process. However, vitamin K_1 is most active in bone health. The nutrient's big selling point is that it is involved in the synthesis of osteocalcin, the major noncollagen protein found in our bones. In simplified terms, vitamin K_1 acts rather like a minister in a marriage ceremony; its presence is necessary for joining together the osteocalcin molecule with calcium and cementing the calcium into place in the bone. Both cortical and trabecular bone contain generous amounts of vitamin K. But with a shortfall of vitamin K_1, bone can become weakened due to insufficient levels of osteocalcin.

Vitamin K_2 has been studied for its value in treating and preventing osteoporosis too, and the scientific landscape is dotted with evidence of the nutrient's influence on bone health. In one study, vitamin K_2 helped prevent the loss of bone mineral from the spine in postmenopausal women. The researchers recommended that vitamin K_2 therapy be started early in the postmenopausal period.

In other research, there's a growing number of such upbeat conclusions regarding these forms of vitamin K. For example:

- Supplemental vitamin K has been shown to increase bone formation in postmenopausal women.

- Low intakes of vitamin K may increase the risk of hip fracture in women, suggesting that higher intakes may protect against these disabling fractures.

- Vitamin K and D may work as partners in reducing bone loss, according to animal research.

What foods are high in vitamin K?
Unless you're strictly a meat-and-potatoes eater, shunting other vegetables to the corner of your plate, it's hard to avoid getting at least some vitamin K in your diet.

The most plentiful dietary sources of vitamin K are unarguably healthful foods: kale, green tea, turnip greens, spinach, broccoli, lettuce, and cabbage.

Should I supplement with vitamin K?

The best way to ensure an adequate intake of vitamin K is to do as your mother probably told you: Eat your vegetables.

The recommended intake is 70 to 150 micrograms daily. Viactiv calcium supplements are fortified with 40 micrograms per chew.

There are no known toxic side effects related to vitamin K supplementation. However, vitamin K supplementation may counteract the actions of blood-thinning drugs such as Coumadin. Inform your doctor if you are taking vitamin K–fortified supplements in case you're prescribed blood-thinners.

VITAMIN C

What does vitamin C do?

When you read about vitamin C, it's usually in reference to its cold-fighting power. But did you also know that vitamin C—the most commonly supplemented nutrient in the United States—can protect bone health as well?

That's right. Vitamin C, also known as ascorbic acid, is a key player in the formation of collagen, the chief protein in bone. Vitamin C is a required cofactor (activator) in biological tasks involving two amino acids, lysine and proline. Both are necessary for the synthesis of collagen.

Interestingly, vitamin C's role in bone health has been known for more than thirty years. In 1967, scientists working in South Africa found that male Bantu laborers suffered from a chronic vitamin C deficiency brought on by "siderosis," a respiratory disease contracted by breathing iron dust. The vitamin C–deficient laborers had all developed osteoporosis. Since the 1970s, several large-scale studies have uncovered a positive link between vitamin C status and bone density. In plain terms: Meet your vitamin C needs, and you may just safeguard your bone health.

More recently, a 1997 study found that women aged 55 to 64 years old who had taken vitamin C supplements for ten years or longer had higher bone mineral densities than women of the same age who had not supplemented. Another study published in 1997 found that dietary vitamin C intake may be linked to greater bone density in the femur. This study was conducted with postmenopausal Mexican American women.

Of course, more research is needed to see how the vitamin C connection to bone health shakes out, but these preliminary findings are intriguing, nonetheless.

For perspective, vitamin C is a water-soluble nutrient that can be synthesized by many animals, but not by humans. In addition to its role in collagen formation, vitamin C is also involved in immunity, wound healing, and allergic responses. As an antioxidant, vitamin C keeps disease-causing molecules called free radicals from destroying the outermost layers of cells.

What foods are high in vitamin C?

The best sources of vitamin C in the diet are citrus fruits and juices. Other foods, such as green and red peppers, collard greens, broccoli, Brussels sprouts, cabbage, spinach, potatoes, cantaloupe, and strawberries are also excellent sources, providing 30 milligrams of vitamin C in a serving of less than 50 calories.

Should I supplement with vitamin C?

So popular is vitamin C that people tend to gobble it by megadoses. Current research shows that taking 250 milligrams a day provides powerful health protection. But if you take 500 milligrams a day, the nutrient can actually promote cell damage and block the body's use of other nutrients. Levels higher than 1,000 milligrams a day can harm your immune system by interfering with the activity of disease-fighting white blood cells. Too much vitamin C makes the body sop up unhealthy amounts of iron and may interfere with the absorption of copper, a trace mineral important to bone health.

Based on these issues, most medical experts advise supplementing with no more than 250 milligrams of vitamin C daily.

VITAMIN B_6 (PYRIDOXINE)

What does vitamin B_6 do?

This B vitamin activates more than one hundred different enzymes, all responsible for hundreds of biochemical tasks. So it's no wonder that vitamin B_6 is involved in bone health.

Specifically, vitamin B_6 is a cofactor (activator) that builds up cross-links, a sort of chemical bridgework that shores up the collagen in your bone. In a 1992 study, researchers in Great Britain discovered that patients with hip fractures were deficient in vitamin B_6. If the body is vitamin B_6-needy, the researchers concluded, it may lack the ability to properly heal fractures.

What foods are high in vitamin B_6?

The best food sources of vitamin B_6 include salmon, Atlantic mackerel, poultry, halibut, tuna, broccoli, lentils, and brown rice.

Should I supplement with vitamin B_6?

The recommended daily intake for vitamin B_6 is 1.6 milligrams—roughly the amount found in the average multivitamin-mineral pill. It's not a good idea to consume over and above the recommended daily intake of vitamin B_6, even as a bone-protective measure, especially since megadoses can be harmful.

9.

How Can I Plan a Bone-Healthy Diet?

To paraphrase an old adage: Your bones are what you eat.

Without a doubt, that means calcium, although not to the exclusion of other nutrients. "The preoccupation to date with calcium has resulted in less emphasis on the role of other nutrients in bone quality and osteoporosis," wrote Ronald G. Munger, et al., in an article published in 1999 in the *American Journal of Clinical Nutrition*.

While there's no question that the case for calcium is stronger than ever, emerging new evidence hints that your total diet, with its array of vitamins, minerals, phytochemicals, and other food factors, may have a more positive effect on osteoporosis than formerly believed.

What follows is a look at some major nutrients and special foods now sharing the center stage with calcium—and how to incorporate them into a bone-healthy diet.

Protein

Dietary protein is used to build bones, organs, nerves, muscles—literally every substance in your body. Protein is made up of subunits called amino acids, which are reshuffled back into protein to make and repair body tissues. Each day, you must eat enough protein to exist, regenerate your body, and stay healthy.

You get protein primarily from animal foods, including calcium-rich dairy foods. Eating animal protein may reduce your odds of hip fracture if you're postmenopausal, according to a recently published study.

Also, protein may help you if you're on the mend from a hip fracture. Supplementation in the form of a protein drink has been shown in research to reduce further bone loss in elderly patients who have suffered hip fractures.

Protein is also found in certain vegetables such as legumes. Plant sources, however, don't contain all the amino acids needed for tissue building. If you're a vegetarian, you must combine plant-based foods carefully so that those lacking in one amino acid are balanced by those sufficient in the same amino acid.

Research hints that protein from vegetable sources is less protective than animal protein against hip fractures. What's more, a comparative study of elderly Chinese vegetarian women and their nonvegetarian counterparts found that bone mineral density in the hip region was significantly lower in vegetarians.

Dietary protein, particularly animal protein, seems to improve bone mineral density, although scientists aren't sure why. One possible clue involves the amino acid lysine. Abundant in animal proteins, lysine is essential for the formation of collagen, the repair of tissue, and the absorption of calcium, among other functions. Other individual amino acids may play a role in strengthening bone too. (In all fairness to plant protein, one group of foods—soy—is bone-protective, according to a growing body of scientific research. More information on that is coming up in this chapter).

There seems to be a fine line between eating too much and too little protein—which is why the exact amount of protein you need for good bone health is controversial. Paradoxically, a high-protein diet improves your body's absorption of calcium, but also increases its excretion.

Insufficient protein is problematic too. One study found that young women who ate a low-protein diet (0.7 grams per kilogram of body weight) for four days had poor calcium absorption and developed hyperparathyroidism as a result. Interestingly, the amount of protein used in the study was only slightly lower than what is normally recommended for adults.

How much protein you eat affects your risk of fracture too. In a study of 85,900 women, those who consumed more than 95 grams of protein a day had an increased risk of forearm fracture than those who ate just 68 grams a day. Among the participants, those who ate five or more servings a week of red meat upped their risk of forearm fracture. By contrast, those who ate red meat less than once a week, on average, had less risk.

It's not clear why the results turned out this way. Perhaps the higher protein intake accelerated calcium losses. Also, red meat is high in saturated fat, which is detrimental to bone health, according to research. Red meat is loaded with phosphorus too. Eating excess phosphorus can cause bone loss.

How much protein should you eat, then?

Nutritional scientists studying the protein-osteoporosis connection believe that a calcium ratio of 20 milligrams of calcium to 1 gram of protein is appropriate for bone health. Using this ratio, an intake of 1,500 milligrams of calcium a day balances out to 75 grams of protein a day—a moderate-protein diet and roughly the amount required in your diet if you're fairly active. For perspective, the equivalent of 75 grams of protein would be: three eight-ounce glasses of skim or soy milk (24 grams), one-half cup of tuna fish (25 grams), and a four-ounce chicken breast (25 grams).

Another way to make sure you eat enough protein: Consume 15 to 20 percent of your total daily calories from protein sources. On a 2,000-calorie-a-day diet, that would compute to 300 to 400 calories of dietary protein.

Carbohydrates

Carbohydrates are bone-friendly foods because they energize you for exercise, and exercise stimulates bone formation and strengthens bones. They are to your body what gas is to a car—the fuel that gets you going. Derived from plants, carbohydrates provide the power for activity and for the growth of all body tissues.

Cereals, pasta, breads, fruits, and vegetables are all examples of carbohydrates. Sugary foods such as candy, cakes, and other processed foods are classified as carbohydrates too, but are less desirable in your diet because of the negligible amount of nutrition they provide.

During digestion, carbohydrates are broken down into blood glucose, also known as blood sugar. Assisted by the hormone insulin, glucose is ushered into cells to be used by various tissues in the body.

Several things can happen to glucose. Once inside a cell, it can be quickly metabolized to supply energy, particularly for the brain and other parts of the nervous system that depend on glucose for fuel. Or it may be converted to either liver or muscle glycogen, the storage form of carbohydrate.

When you exercise or use your muscles, the body mobilizes muscle glycogen for energy. If you lack the get-up-and-go to exercise, your body may be running low on carbohydrates.

Glucose can also turn into body fat and get packed away in fat tissue. This happens when you eat more carbohydrates than you need or than your body can store as liver or muscle glycogen.

Besides providing the energy for bone-building exercise, carbohydrates may have another anti-osteoporosis benefit. They contain food factors called fructooligosaccharides, naturally occurring but indigestible sugars found in such foods as bananas, garlic, barley, onion, wheat, and tomatoes. In scientific experiments mostly with rats, fructooligosaccharides have been shown to increase the absorption of calcium and magnesium, promote bone strength, and prevent the loss of bone density. To date, two fructooligosaccharide studies with humans also showed a positive effect, increasing calcium absorption by 26 to 58 percent.

Certainly, the case for fructooligosaccharides as osteoporosis therapy isn't yet proved, but they appear promising nonetheless. Populating your diet with more carbohydrates is a good move anyway, since they furnish such a smorgasbord of beneficial nutrients.

Carbohydrates such as fruits and vegetables are rich in potassium and magnesium—two minerals known to help prevent osteoporosis. In a study of 1,164 men and women over a four-year period, a high intake of fruits and vegetables was positively associated with good bone health. Potatoes, bananas, and orange juice are high in potassium. Good sources of magnesium include skim milk, whole grains, bananas, and orange juice.

Ideally, 60 to 65 percent of the calories in your daily diet should come from carbohydrates, particularly natural carbohydrates. If you eat 2,000 calories a day, for example, 1,200 to 1,300 calories would come from carbohydrates. The best way to increase natural carbohydrates is to add foods like fruit, whole-grain cereals and breads, rice, potatoes, yams, and plenty of vegetables to your diet.

Fats

Dietary fat is an essential nutrient, required to help form the structures of cell membranes, regulate metabolism, and provide a source of energy for exercise and activity.

There are three types of dietary fat, classified according to their hydrogen content: saturated, monounsaturated, and polyunsaturated. Saturated fats are usually solid at room temperature and, with the exception of tropical oils, come from animal sources. Beef fat and butterfat are high in saturated fats, while low-fat or skimmed milk products are much lower in saturated fat. Tropical oils high in saturated fat include coconut oil, palm kernel oil, palm oil, and the cocoa fat found in chocolate. They are generally found in commercial baked goods and other processed foods.

Studies in animals have found that diets high in saturated fat block the absorption of calcium, weaken the skeleton, and degrade trabecular bone. Researchers believe that such diets may also be detrimental to human bones.

Polyunsaturated and monounsaturated fats are usually liquid at room temperature and come from nut, vegetable, or seed sources. Monounsaturated fats are found in large amounts in olive oil, canola oil, and peanut oil, and in fish from cold waters, such as salmon, mackerel, halibut, swordfish, black cod, and rainbow trout, and in shellfish.

Technically, the maximum amount of fat considered healthy in your daily diet is 30 percent or less of the number of calories you eat. On a 2,000-calorie-a-day diet, for instance, fat intake would equal 600 calories. Saturated fat should be 10 percent or less of total daily calories; monounsaturated and polyunsaturated fats should also be 10 percent or less.

Special Bone-Building Foods: Phytoestrogens

Nature has given us a virtual cornucopia of health-giving nutrients in our foods. Now scientists have discovered some new components in foods that have some amazing disease-fighting powers. They're called *phyto-chemicals,* which means "plant chemicals."

The food you eat contains thousands of these chemicals. Unlike vitamins and minerals, phytochemicals don't have any nutritive value, but they do seem to protect against cancer, heart disease, and other illnesses.

The search for safer, better-tolerated alternatives to hormone replacement therapy (HRT) has thrust phyto-chemicals called *phytoestrogens* into the nutritional spotlight. Phytoestrogens are generally categorized into three groups:

- Isoflavones, plentiful in soy foods and other legumes.

- Lignans, a constituent of the cell walls of plants. Lignans are found in a wide variety of fruits and vegetables, but are especially concentrated in flaxseed.

- Coumestans, an important source of natural estrogen for animals, though not for humans. These compounds are found in fodder crops such as alfalfa. They are also highly concentrated in bean sprouts.

ISOFLAVONES AND YOUR HEALTH

Of the three, isoflavones confer the greatest health benefits, particularly to menopausal and postmenopausal women. During these life stages, less estrogen is available to enter the body's cells. Cells, however, recognize isoflavones as estrogen. They gain entry to cells, just as estrogen does, through "cellular receptors." Mounted on cell membranes, these receptors are like door buzzers, signaling the cell to open up and let certain substances in. Isoflavones enter the cell, where they increase levels of estrogen.

Until fairly recently, isoflavones were thought to be weak estrogens because they didn't latch on to receptors as well as bodily estrogen does. Scientists, however, have discovered that many isoflavones are much stronger than your body's own estrogen. This simply means that the isoflavones attach to receptors without any problem. The cell opens right up, welcoming the isoflavones in.

Because isoflavones look and act like estrogen, they provide a natural, less risky source of estrogen—which is why many postmenopausal women are forgoing hor-

mone replacement therapy (HRT) in favor of a
phytoestrogen-rich diet. Long-term HRT can increase
the risk of breast cancer and is becoming a concern
among women and physicians. By contrast, dietary
sources of isoflavones—namely, soybeans and other legumes—are associated with decreased risk of breast cancer, improved cholesterol profiles, and beneficial effects
on bone density.

ISOFLAVONES AND BONE DENSITY

Are isoflavones good bone-builders? At least two human studies say yes.

In one of these studies, sixty-six postmenopausal
women took one of two doses of soy isoflavones (they
are available as supplements): either 55.6 milligrams a
day or 90 milligrams a day for six months. There was
also a control group.

Here's what happened: Bone mineral density and
bone mineral content in the spine increased significantly
in the women who supplemented with 90 milligrams a
day of soy isoflavones.

In the other study, researchers looked into the bone-
protective effects of isoflavones. Thirty postmenopausal
women—none had osteoporosis—supplemented with either 60 grams a day of soy protein or 60 grams a day
of casein, a milk protein. The experimental period lasted
three months.

The research team examined urine samples to detect
the presence of two compounds that indicate bone degeneration. In the soy-supplemented women, there were
declines in the excretion of these chemicals—which
means that less bone was being torn down. This finding
hints at a protective effect of soy protein.

Two types of isoflavones are believed to build bone density and protect bone health: daidzein and genistein. Found in soy foods, daidzein appears to promote bone formation. Soy foods cause less calcium to be excreted in urine, and scientists think daidzein may be the reason why. If so, eating soy foods could certainly be another hedge against osteoporosis and its progression.

Genistein is one of the more stronger-acting phytoestrogens—which means it is easily attracted to certain receptors and thus gains fast access to cells. But less is known about genistein's effect on bone health. However, genistein is structurally similar to a synthetic compound called ipriflavone (see chapter 10), which prevents bone degeneration. Because of ipriflavone's similarity to genistein, scientists theorize that genistein may also be bone protective. Soy foods are rich in genistein.

It's important to point out that Japanese women, who consume a soy-rich diet throughout life, have a reduced risk of hip fracture, according to research. Isoflavone-rich soy foods are believed to be a key reason why.

Clearly, a good move is to include more soy products in your diet, particularly as substitutes for meat or milk in low-fat cooking. Be aware, however, that the phytoestrogen content of soy foods varies from product to product. A study from Tufts University School of Medicine showed that tofu contains high amounts of the isoflavones genistein and daidzein, but the content varies slightly among brands. Some dietary supplements formulated from what's known as "isolated soy protein" contain no phytoestrogens at all. Read labels to be sure of what you're getting.

In addition to phytoestrogens, soy foods contain all the amino acids (protein components) needed by the body. Plus, they're an excellent source of iron, B vitamins, calcium, zinc, and dietary fiber.

Some of the more popular soy foods include miso (a condiment used in soups), soy cheese, soy flour, soy milk, tempeh, and tofu.

Special Bone-Building Foods: Whey Protein

When Little Miss Muffet sat down to eat her curds and whey, she was dining on a very bone-healthy meal—high in calcium and rich in protein. But it's the whey portion of her meal that deserves special mention.

Whey is a component of milk that is separated out during the process of making cheese and other dairy products. More recently, it is a chief ingredient of some protein powders and drinks sold in health food stores.

Recent scientific evidence shows that whey plays a role in bone formation. In one experiment, some amazing things happened after whey was introduced into osteoblasts (cells that form bone). The protein content of the cells increased, and protein is a building material for tissue, including bone. Also, the amount of hydroxyproline increased. Hydroxyproline is a constituent of collagen, a connective tissue found in bone.

Further, the content of genetic material in cells increased—another indicator of growth. The investigators who conducted this experiment speculate that whey protein activates osteoblasts to trigger growth. These findings have potentially far-reaching implications in the treatment of osteoporosis and other bone diseases.

Whey has other well-known talents. First, it's rich in calcium and other minerals. Plus, it's well endowed with the milk sugar lactose, which helps your body absorb calcium.

Whey is also high in B-complex vitamins—a family of nutrients that work in accord to ensure proper digestion, muscle contraction, and energy production. Whey is particularly rich in vitamin B_{12}, which is vital to healthy blood and a normal nervous system. It works together with folic acid to form red blood cells in the bone marrow.

What's more, whey increases levels of glutathione in the body. Glutathione is a peptide (an amino acid combination) that works inside cells as a natural antioxidant to strengthen immunity against disease. It also helps remove toxic cellular by-products from the body. The elevation of glutathione has been shown to inhibit the development of several types of tumors, according to numerous studies. So vital is glutathione that without it, you would die.

It's easy to incorporate whey into your diet. Prepare a shake consisting of whey protein powder, water or juice, and some cut-up fruit. Drink between meals as a healthy, refreshing snack.

Special Bone-Building Foods: Tea

Even though high caffeine intake is a risk factor for low bone density, sipping some tea daily may prevent bone loss. So says a study from England that involved more than twelve hundred women, aged 65 to 76.

The women were divided into two groups—tea drinkers and non-tea drinkers. All of the women had their bone density measured in the lumbar spine, as well as in the femoral neck, greater trochanter, and Ward's triangle (areas where hip breaks occur most often). Among tea drinkers, even those who drank coffee, bone density and strength was significantly greater. Adding milk to tea boosted the bone-protective benefit even more.

Researchers aren't exactly sure why drinking tea does your bones so much good. They think it may have something to do with nutrients in tea called flavonoids, which weakly mimic the action of estrogen, a bone-protective hormone. Quit possibly, flavonoids may negate the harmful effects of caffeine on bones.

Green tea may ward off osteoporosis too, according to research conducted in Asia, where it is a dietary staple. Green tea is rich in vitamin K (see page 120), which helps guard against osteoporosis.

Unless you're sensitive to caffeine, you may want to drink tea to help fight osteoporosis.

Planning a Bone-Healthy Diet

Plan your diet so that you get most of your calories from grain products, vegetables, fruits, low-fat diary products, lean meats, fish, poultry, and dry beans. Choose fewer calories from fats and sweets. High-sugar diets rob your body of vitamins and minerals.

Eat a variety of foods. Foods contain combinations of nutrients and other healthful substances. No single food can supply all nutrients in the amounts you need.

The United States Department of Agriculture has created excellent dietary guidelines for Americans, and these guidelines help ensure that you obtain maximum nutrition from your meals. Here's how you can plan your meals according to the food groups established by the Department of Agriculture.

Bread, cereal, rice, and pasta (6–11 servings daily)
One serving equals:

- 1 slice of bread
- 1 ounce of ready-to-eat cereal
- ½ cup of cooked cereal, rice, or pasta

If you're on a weight-reducing diet, you may want to decrease the number of carbohydrate servings in your diet—possibly by half. Lower-carbohydrates diets enhance weight loss.

Vegetables (3–5 servings daily)
One serving equals:

- 1 cup of raw leafy vegetables
- ½ cup of other vegetables, cooked or chopped raw
- ¾ cup of vegetable juice

Vegetables are loaded with health-building nutrients. Try to eat a variety of vegetables in a variety of colors. Choose dark, leafy green vegetables, deep-yellow or orange vegetables, and starchy vegetables such as potatoes, sweet potatoes, and yams.

Fruits (2–3 servings daily)
One serving equals:

- 1 medium apple, banana, or orange
- ½ cup of chopped, cooked, canned, or frozen fruit
- ¾ cup of fruit juice

Fruits are another food packed with health-building nutrients. Your best choices are fresh fruits and juices, and frozen or dried fruits.

Milk, yogurt, and cheese (2–3 servings daily)
One serving equals:

- 1 cup of skim milk, soy milk, or low-fat or nonfat yogurt

- 2 ounces of processed low-fat or nonfat cheese, tofu, or cottage cheese

Choose low-fat varieties to keep saturated fat in check. Saturated fat, found in animal foods, is responsible for elevating dangerous cholesterol in the body and may be detrimental to bone health.

Meat, poultry, fish, dry beans, eggs, nuts, and seeds (2–3 servings daily)
One serving equals:

- 2–3 ounces of cooked lean meat, poultry, or fish

- ½ cup of cooked dry beans

- 1 egg

- 2 egg whites

- 2 tablespoons nuts or seeds

Select low-fat varieties of animal proteins such as lean red meat, white meat poultry, and fish.

Fats, oils, and sweets
Choose these foods sparingly.

As you can see, these guidelines provide a range of servings for each food group. The smaller number is for people who consume about 1,600 calories a day, such as many sedentary women do. The larger number is for those who consume about 2,800 calories a day and are more active.

Notice too that some of the serving sizes are smaller than what you might usually eat. For example, many people eat a cup or more of rice in a meal, which equals two or more servings. Thus, it is easy to eat the number of servings recommended.

Some foods fit into more than one group. Dry beans, peas, and lentils can be counted as servings in either the meat and beans group or the vegetables group.

10.

What Medicines Are Available to Treat Osteoporosis?

At this time, the only drugs approved by the FDA for treating osteoporosis are estrogen, alendronate (Fosamax), calcitonin, and raloxifene (Evista). Other drugs are under consideration, with some already being used to treat the disease. The major anti-osteoporosis medicines are described below. You should discuss these medications with your physician.

FDA-Approved Agents for Osteoporosis

HORMONE REPLACEMENT THERAPY (HRT)

HRT involves treatment with estrogen, often along with progestin (a synthetic progesterone). Estrogen is recommended for women at risk of osteoporosis because replacing estrogen lost at menopause helps maintain and strengthen bone. Estrogen is an "antiresorptive agent."

It inhibits bone breakdown by osteoclasts (bone resorption) and thus slows the rate of bone loss.

The hormone progestin is given with estrogen if you have not had a hysterectomy. Estrogen taken by itself greatly increases the risk of uterine cancer. Progestin offsets that risk.

If you are postmenopausal, HRT is considered to be the first-choice drug therapy for maintaining bone mass and reducing your risk of fracture. It comes in various forms: oral, transdermal patches, vaginal creams, vaginal rings, and gel (available in Europe and Canada only).

HRT has an excellent track record of reducing the risk of bone fractures due to osteoporosis. For example, with five years of use, HRT can decrease your chance of a spinal fracture by 50 to 80 percent and your chance of a nonspinal fracture by 25 percent. With ten or more years of use, HRT can reduce your risk of all fractures by 50 to 75 percent.

Who should take HRT?
Currently, HRT is recommended if:

- You have multiple osteoporosis risk factors, such as early menopause, a blood relative with osteoporosis, or low bone density (osteopenia).

- Your ovaries were removed before age 50.

- You experienced natural menopause before age 50.

- You have been diagnosed with established, or severe, osteoporosis.

- You desire HRT for its other possible benefits, such as protection against heart disease. (*Please note, however, that a major, long-term study of postmenopausal women with heart disease—the Estrogen Replacement and Atherosclerosis Study—demonstrated that HRT did not slow the course of the disease.*)

For preventing osteoporosis, HRT works best if begun just after the onset of menopause and maintained for at least ten years. However, research shows that HRT reduces the risk of hip fracture, even when therapy is initiated nine or more years following the onset of menopause.

What is the usual dosage?
For the treatment of osteoporosis in the United States, dosages for HRT are listed below.

TABLE 10.1
HRT Drug Dosages

Preparation	Dosage
Estrace*	0.5 mg a day (administered cyclically, 23 days on and 5 days off)
Estraderm*	0.05 mg delivered daily via a skin patch that should be replaced twice a week
Ogen*	0.625 mg a day
Premarin*	0.625 mg a day (administered cyclically, 3 weeks on and 1 week off)
Premphase	0.625 mg (estrogen) with 5 mg (progestin) a day

PremPro   0.625 mg (estrogen) with
                                2.5 mg (progestin) a day

*These drugs are estrogen-only preparations, which are usually pre-
scribed with progestin in women who still have their uteruses.
    Adapted from: Genant, H. K., G. Guglielmi, and M. Jergas. (eds.). 1998.
    Bone densitometry and osteoporosis. New York: Springer.*

At what point should HRT be stopped?
Consult your physician about when, or if, to discontinue
therapy. When HRT is discontinued, bone loss often accelerates. However, with prolonged use of HRT, the protective effect of estrogen against spinal and hip fractures
subsides.

What are the potential side effects?
Worrisome side effects include vaginal bleeding, water
retention, breast pain and tenderness, nausea, headaches,
gallbladder disease, and mood disturbances. More serious risks include increased risk of uterine cancer if not
combined with progestin; deep vein thrombosis; and
breast cancer.

How serious is the risk of breast cancer?
With long-term use (ten or more years) HRT has been
associated with a modest increase in the risk of breast
cancer. Short-term use (under five years) is not associated with an elevated risk.

What if you use HRT for five to ten years? At this
point, the scientific evidence is less clear, but there may
be a slightly elevated risk.

It is important to point out that one of the top factors
in the risk of breast cancer is advancing age. Approxi-

mately 90 percent of all breast cancer cases occur in women who have never taken estrogen—which is why many physicians concur that the benefits of HRT outweigh its risks.

How can side effects be minimized?

Your physician can customize the dosage to minimize side effects or to bring about desired health benefits. It's usually better to begin with the lowest dose first and modify the dosage depending on how you respond.

If you're experiencing side effects, your physician may also prescribe a different brand of HRT or recommend a different delivery system.

Many side effects can be nipped in the bud by basic lifestyle changes. For instance, you can curtail nausea by taking your HRT pill at bedtime, counteract bloating by restricting your salt intake, or ease breast tenderness by cutting down on caffeine. Keep your physician informed about any and all side effects.

ALENDRONATE (FOSAMAX)

Alendronate is a member of a large group of compounds known as bisphosphonates. Bisphosphonates cling to mineral in the bone and, in effect, shut out the osteoclasts. This action sabotages the osteoclasts' job, which is to break down bone. Like estrogen, alendronate is an antiresorptive agent.

Alendronate performs impressively as an agent to prevent and treat osteoporosis. This medication has been shown to:

- Reduce the incidence of fractures at the spine, hip, and wrist by 50 percent in patients with osteoporosis.

- Reduce the risk of new spinal and hip fractures by about 50 percent in women diagnosed with low bone mineral density.

- Slow the progression of spinal deformities associated with osteoporosis.

- Prevent loss of height caused by osteoporosis.

Who should take alendronate?
Medical experts feel that alendronate is as effective as HRT in treating osteoporosis. Alendronate is a nonhormonal agent, and thus a powerful alternative if you are unwilling or unable to take hormone replacement therapy.

Alendronate is prescribed if you are postmenopausal, with low bone density or at risk for osteoporosis. Whether the drug remains effective and safe beyond a four-year period is not known. Nor do medical experts know how discontinuing treatment affects the rate of bone loss.

What is the usual dose?
Available in tablets, alendronate is prescribed in 5-milligram doses for the prevention of osteoporosis; in 10-milligram doses for its treatment.

Take it on an empty stomach, first thing in the morning, with a large glass of water, about thirty minutes prior to eating. You should remain upright over the next hour. This helps prevent a reaction in which the drug is expelled into the esophagus from the stomach.

Do not take alendronate at the same time you take your calcium supplement. Calcium supplements block the absorption of alendronate.

What are the potential side effects?
Although well tolerated, alendronate can sometimes cause headache, stomach pain, and irritation of the esophagus, according the *Physicians' Desk Reference*.

CALCITONIN

Another FDA-approved agent for the treatment of osteoporosis is salmon calcitonin, a hormone derived from salmon. It is a synthetic form of calcitonin, a naturally occurring hormone produced by the thyroid gland.

Calcitonin's main effect in the body is to interfere with the activity of osteoclasts and shorten their lifespan. This action enables bone to retain more calcium and keeps it from becoming brittle.

Medical studies show that calcitonin:

- May decrease the incidence of osteoporosis-related spinal fractures by approximately 40 percent.

- Retards bone loss in women even if started five years after menopause.

- May relieve the pain often felt in osteoporosis, possibly by increasing the body's level of endorphins, natural feel-good chemicals that bring on a sense of well-being.

Who should take calcitonin?
Calcitonin slows bone loss in women who are at least five years beyond menopause. Therefore, it should not be prescribed during the first five years after menopause.

Calcitonin is an alternative drug if you cannot or will not take HRT or a bisphosphonate such as alendronate.

Medical experts have not yet identified an optimal duration of treatment.

What is the usual dosage?

Calcitonin is digested in the stomach and therefore cannot be taken orally. Instead, it is delivered as a single daily nasal spray (Miacalcin nasal spray) that provides 200 units of the drug.

Calcitonin is recommended in conjunction with adequate calcium (at least 1,000 milligrams daily) and vitamin D (400 IU daily) to help slow down the rate of bone loss.

Calcitonin is also available as an injectable drug (Miaclacin and Calcimar).

What are the potential side effects?

Side effects may include allergic reactions and nasal irritation, according to the *Physicians' Desk Reference.*

RALOXIFENE (EVISTA)

This drug is a member of a class of compounds called selective estrogen receptor modulators (SERMs), which provide the benefits of estrogen, but without its side effects. Marketed as Evista, raloxifene is thus another viable option for the prevention of postmenopausal osteoporosis.

Although it is yet unclear exactly how raloxifene works, the drug prevents bone resorption and has estrogenlike effects on bone that result in beefed-up bone density. Preliminary data on raloxifene indicates that it can reduce the risk of spinal fractures by 40 to 50 percent.

A fascinating finding about raloxifene is that it may prevent breast cancer. This encouraging news was found in a large-scale study of women with osteoporosis. The study demonstrated a 76 percent reduction in the incidence of breast cancer.

Who should take raloxifene?
This drug is beneficial if you:

- Are at moderate risk for osteoporosis

- Can't or won't use HRT

- Have infrequent hot flashes

- Are at low risk for cardiovascular disease

- Are at a moderate to high risk of breast cancer

What is the usual dose?
Raloxifene is taken orally in tablet form. The recommended dosage is one 60-milligram tablet daily. You can take raloxifene at any time during the day, with or without meals.

What are the potential side effects?
Side effects include hot flashes and increased risk of deep vein thrombosis, according to the *Physicians' Desk Reference*.

COMBINED TREATMENTS

Your physician may prescribe a combination of agents, depending on the state of your bone health. Scientifically, there is strong rationale for this approach. Consider:

- HRT plus a non-FDA-approved bisphosphonate called etidronate (Didronel) was found to preserve and enhance bone mineral density in postmenopausal women with severe osteoporosis over a four-year period. In addition, all patients took 1,000 milligrams of calcium and 400 IU of vitamin D daily. Those women who took the combined therapy had significantly higher bone mineral density in their spine and femur than those patients who took HRT or etidronate alone.

- HRT taken in combination with alendronate is an effective therapy too. In a study of women who had had hysterectomies and had been diagnosed with osteoporosis, the combined regimen increased spine and femoral neck bone mineral density more than either drug alone.

How Do I Select a Treatment That's Best for Me?

Clearly, there are a number of beneficial agents available for preventing and treating osteoporosis. But which one is best for you?

In general, HRT and alendronate promote the greatest increases in bone density, but may not be appropriate for every case. If you're concerned about your risk of breast cancer, for example, you may not want to undergo

HRT. On the other hand, if you want to possibly reduce your risk of heart disease—and treat osteoporosis at the same time—you may want to pursue HRT. Or, you may want to choose another course altogether, such as a natural therapy.

Your treatment should be tailored toward your degree of bone loss, your T-score, your fracture risk, and your personal concerns about the risk of breast cancer versus that of heart disease. These issues should be discussed with your physician, who can help you weigh the risks and benefits associated with various therapies. You may even want to consider taking ipriflavone, a synthetic compound derived from the soy isoflavone daidzein. (For information on ipriflavone, see page 157.)

Are There Other Drugs That Treat Osteoporosis?

Several other drugs, in fact, treat osteoporosis, but they are not approved by the FDA for that purpose. These agents should be mentioned, however, because you may hear about them and have questions. Some physicians prescribe them. Non-FDA-approved drugs include the following:

Sodium fluoride
Sodium fluoride is a trace mineral required by the body in small amounts. (For more information on how fluoride works in the body, see chapter 8.) Through a mechanism that is yet unclear, sodium fluoride stimulates the formation of new bone. However, the quality of the newly formed bone mass is questionable. It has an abnormal texture, less mineral, and is somewhat fragile.

Further, there is conflicting data over whether sodium fluoride reduces the risk of fractures.

Calcitriol

Calcitriol is a synthetic "twin" of vitamin D that promotes calcium absorption. A problem with calcitriol, however, is that it stimulates the activity of bone-breaking osteoclasts and thus could lead to reduced bone mass. Using calcitriol to treat osteoporosis is iffy at best, since treatment could be beneficial or harmful.

What's more, research into the use of calcitriol to treat osteoporosis has produced disappointing results. In three studies, researchers discovered that it actually accelerated the rate of vertebral height loss.

At present, calcitriol seems unsuitable as a treatment for osteoporosis. It is approved by the FDA, however, for managing hypocalcemia (abnormally low blood calcium levels) and metabolic bone disease in kidney dialysis patients. It is also prescribed to treat low calcium levels in people who have hypoparathyroidism (abnormal function of the parathyroid glands). When functioning normally, the parathyroid glands help regulate the amount of calcium in the blood.

Other bisphosphonates

These agents belong to the same family as alendronate. They include etidronate, tiludronate, risedronate, pamidronate, and ibandronate. Many are used to treat various bone diseases.

Etidronate (Didronel) is approved for the treatment of osteoporosis in several countries, including Canada. The FDA United States has not approved it because a study with four hundred osteoporotic patients found that although etidronate increased spinal and hip bone density by 5 and 3 percent respectively, it did not significantly reduce the incidence of fracture.

Tiludronate and inbandronate are being clinically evaluated for their effects on osteoporosis.

Thiazide diuretics

These drugs are prescribed to treat high blood pressure (hypertension) and other conditions that require the elimination of excess water from the body. Thiazide diuretics prevent urinary losses of calcium, and some studies show that hypertensive people who take these drugs have increased bone mass and a reduced risk of hip fractures.

However, many medical experts feel that this could be a coincidence—for one reason. People with high blood pressure tend to have a higher body weight, which often leads to greater bone mass. Even so, thiazide diuretics are being talked about as a preventive measure against osteoporosis. At present though, thiazide diuretics are not considered a viable treatment for osteoporosis.

Anabolic steroids

A class of therapeutic agents sometimes regarded as beneficial in promoting new bone formation is anabolic steroids. Generally, these drugs are synthetic male hormones (usually testosterone), approved to help develop or maintain male sex characteristics in men or boys whose bodies are not producing enough testosterone on their own.

Anabolic steroids used in osteoporosis therapy are testosterone analogs—chemical twins of testosterone that have been modified to reduce their masculinizing effects. These agents do produce positive changes in bone density, but often with troubling side effects. These include the development of acne, unwanted hair growth, and voice changes.

Promising New Treatments

Scientists are working in earnest on newer, better treatments for osteoporosis, and the good news is, they're close. Within several years, expect to see a whole new arsenal of agents to fight the disease—and, best of all, to fully prevent new fractures once the disease has taken hold (no current medicines have this ability).

At present, most osteoporosis drugs are "antiresorptive," meaning they inhibit the activity of osteoclasts. Those on the horizon, however, are geared toward stimulating the activity of osteoblasts. The following is a crystal-ball glimpse into the future of osteoporosis treatment.

Statins
An agent that stimulates bone formation and inhibits bone resorption would certainly be a great breakthrough in the treatment of osteoporosis. Statins just might be it.

Statins are a class of drugs approved for lowering cholesterol levels in the blood of patients with primary hypercholesterolemia (too much cholesterol). Now it appears that statins could be developed into a new treatment for osteoporosis.

Scientists have recently discovered that statins can stimulate new bone formation. They also decrease the number of osteoclasts on bone surfaces. Thus, statins can build bone and possibly prevent its breakdown. Although more research is needed, the possibilities are intriguing.

Parathyroid peptides

Scientists believe that parathyroid peptides may have the power to increase the replication rate and the lifespan of osteoblasts, thus increasing their number. To date, preliminary studies indicate that parathyroid peptides:

- Increase trabecular bone mass.

- Prevent bone loss in the lumbar spine.

- Increase bone mineral density.

Strontium ranelate

Strontium is a metallic trace element that was proposed for the treatment of osteoporosis more than thirty-five years ago. In a study of postmenopausal women with osteoporosis, strontium ranelate (2 grams daily) taken orally caused a significant increase in bone mineral density in the lumbar spine.

Strontium may work as a preventive measure too. In another study—this one conducted with early postmenopausal women without osteoporosis—strontium (1 gram daily) increased bone mineral density in the spine and hip.

Growth hormone

Stored in the pituitary gland and secreted throughout your lifetime, growth hormone is involved in the growth of body tissues and is involved in the metabolism of protein, carbohydrates, and fats.

As a synthetic drug, growth hormone is typically prescribed to growth hormone–deficient children to stimulate normal growth. Now it's being studied as a possible treatment for severe osteoporosis. In studies with animals and humans, it stimulates bone remodeling—the process of replacing old bone with new bone through the activity of osteoblasts and osteoclasts.

Ipriflavone: A Natural Medicine to Consider

Suppose you're opposed to taking any prescription medicine. What recourse do you have?

You might consider ipriflavone, a pill that blocks the breakdown of bone *and* builds it up—but without the worrisome side effects of estrogen and other prescription anti-osteoporosis drugs.

Ipriflavone is a rather amazing agent derived from a soy isoflavone, daidzein. It holds great promise for preventing and treating osteoporosis.

Ipriflavone was discovered in the 1930s, but not synthesized until 1969. At that time, it was used as a feed additive for veterinary applications.

In 1988, Japanese medical authorities registered ipriflavone as a drug called Osten. European countries, as well as Argentina, followed Japan's example. In the United States, however, ipriflavone is available as a dietary supplement. Although ipriflavone is a synthetic isoflavone, it is found in nature in bee propolis, a resin collected by bees from the buds of trees, mixed with their wax, and used to line beehives.

In the last decade, there have been more than sixty well-controlled human studies on ipriflavone's ability to prevent and reverse bone loss. This extensive body of research shows that ipriflavone is not only safe, but also effective for the treatment of osteoporosis. Human studies indicate that ipriflavone:

- Arrests bone loss in postmenopausal patients and others who are at risk for developing osteoporosis.

- Increases the amount of calcium warehoused in the bones.

- Works with calcium to improve bone density. Studies show that postmenopausal women who take 600 milligrams of ipriflavone a day, along with 500 milligrams of calcium a day, can increase or maintain bone density in their arms and spine.

- Prevents the loss of bone mineral density in the spine. In a two-year study, 198 women took either 200 milligrams of ipriflavone three times a day, along with 1 gram of calcium—or only calcium and a placebo (look-alike pill). After six months of ipriflavone-calcium supplementation, spinal bone mineral density increased 1.4 percent—which is clinically significant and lowers the risk of fracture.

- Protects against the rapid loss of bone density often experienced within the first five years of menopause.

- May fight Type II osteoporosis (senile osteoporosis) in women over age 70. In a two-year study of twenty-eight elderly women (aged 65 to 79) with osteoporosis, researchers found that 200 milligrams (three times a day) and 1 gram of calcium (once a day) boosted bone mineral density by 6 percent after one year.

- Helps reduce the incidence of fractures. In a two-year study of eighty-four subjects, half the group took 200 milligrams of ipriflavone three times a day, and the other half took 1 gram of calcium a day. The results were intriguing: Two of forty-one patients suffered fractures in the ipriflavone group, whereas eleven of forty-three patients experienced fractures in the calcium-only group.

- Relieves bone pain associated with osteoporosis.

- Is effective in the prevention of bone loss due to disease- or medication-induced osteoporosis (secondary osteoporosis).

How, exactly, does ipriflavone work this magic? In several ways—all of which appear to enhance bone density.

To begin with, ipriflavone is rather unique among osteoporosis treatments. Here's why: Most drugs approved for treating osteoporosis are antiresorptive; that is, they inhibit the activity of osteoclasts, which break down bone. Antiresorptive agents include estrogen, calcium, alendronate, and calcitonin. Ipriflavone appears to inhibit osteoclast activity *and* to stimulate the activity of osteoblasts.

In addition, ipriflavone increases the body's uptake of bone-building calcium. It also appears to increase the secretion of calcitonin, a naturally occurring hormone involved in building bone.

The chemical structure of ipriflavone resembles that of estrogen, and consequently, the body recognizes it as estrogen. But like a copycat, it mimics the action of estrogen, without producing estrogen's untoward side effects.

If you take hormone replacement therapy, you may be able to get by with a lower dose by supplementing with ipriflavone. That's because ipriflavone works well in partnership with other osteoporosis treatments. A number of studies have found that ipriflavone enhances the effect of low-dose estrogen on bone preservation. In medical experiments, the daily dosage shown to be most effective in increasing bone mineral density is 600 milligrams of ipriflavone and 0.30 milligrams of estrogen.

At least one study has compared the effects of ipriflavone with those of calcitonin, an antiresorptive drug approved for the treatment of osteoporosis. After twelve months of therapy, there was a 4.3 percent increase in bone mineral density in the ipriflavone group and a 1.9 increase in the calcitonin group. Forty postmenopausal women participated in the study. This study suggests that ipriflavone may be an effective alternative to calcitonin therapy.

Numerous supplement companies manufacture ipriflavone and ipriflavone-containing formulas: Solgar Vitamin and Herbs, Schiff (Weider Nutrition), Natural Balance, Advanced Nutritional Products, and Natrol.

The recommended dose is 200 milligrams, taken three times a day. Ipriflavone is best taken after a meal, because food greatly improves its absorption.

However, Ipriflavone can raise liver enzymes slightly. This means it could interfere with your body's ability to metabolize certain drugs. If you take ipriflavone while on medication, ask your doctor to do blood tests on a regular basis.

If you're using or considering ipriflavone, discuss your decision with your physician. That way, your use of natural medicine can be coordinated with the conventional care you are receiving from your physician.

Some Final Words on Treatment

Taking anti-osteoporosis medicine is not a substitute for healthy lifestyle practices, such as diet and exercise.

While undergoing treatment, make sure you're following a bone-healthy diet, consuming enough calcium and other bone-building nutrients, and engaging in weight-bearing exercise. In the next chapter, you'll learn how to design a bone-density workout that's right for you.

11.

What Kind of Exercise Promotes Bone Density?

You work out to stay trim or lose weight, but have you ever considered exercising for the sake of your bones?

Certain types of exercise guard against bone loss and build bone mass. That's good news if you're concerned about age-related bone loss or personal risk factors for osteoporosis. Plus, if you've never been very active, now is the time to get moving. Inactivity depletes bone mineral. It's never too late to start replenishing it either.

There is an enormous body of other data proving that exercise builds bone and makes it stronger. Consider a few of the findings:

- After completing an eight-month exercise program, women aged 50 to 72 upped the bone mineral content in their lower spines by 3.5 percent.

- Athletic women aged 55 to 72 had higher bone mineral density values than nonathletic women in the same age group. In fact, several studies indicate that bone density is 25 percent greater in athletes than in regular exercisers, and 30 percent greater in regular exercisers than in couch potatoes.

- Women who have engaged in weight-bearing exercise (including household and work-related activity) all their lives have high bone mineral density throughout their bodies.

How does exercise build bone density?

Exercise has a near-miraculous effect on bone density. With exercise, your bones respond the same way your muscles do—they get bigger and stronger. That's because you're placing stress on them. Like muscle, bone adapts to stress by becoming stronger. At the cellular level, bone cells start multiplying and producing more bone.

Without this type of stress, bones wither and waste away—as do muscles. In fact, inactivity reduces the activity of bone-forming osteoblasts, leading to a loss of bone.

Researchers have observed this phenomenon in tennis players and other athletes. A right-handed tennis player, for example, has about 30 percent more bone in the right arm than in the left, which doesn't get exercised as much.

In addition, muscle contraction—the flexing and unflexing of your muscles—builds bone mass too. Muscles are attached to joints, the structure where the ends of bone meet. When muscles contract, joints move, operating like hinges on a door or a joystick on a video game. The movement of the muscles and joints exerts a rotational force, or pull, on the bones, called torque. The greater the torque, the stronger the bones.

Another key point is this: With age-related muscle loss—usually brought on by inactivity—calcium exits from your body. That's because muscle loss forces nitrogen (a constituent of muscle) out of the body. When nitrogen goes, so does bone-strengthening calcium. By preserving muscle, exercise prevents this harmful exodus.

What type of exercise is best?

In a nutshell, weight training is the best exercise for strengthening bone. With weight training, you apply resistance—in the form of dumbbells, barbells, weight training machines, or other special equipment—against your muscles. Examples of weight training include lifting weights, working out on weight-training machines, performing calisthenics, and exercising with special rubber bands.

A study at the University of Arizona looked at groups of women aged 17 to 38. Some were bodybuilders; others were competitive runners; and still others were swimmers and recreational runners. For comparison, a control group was made up of women who did not exercise. When measured, the average bone mineral content of the bodybuilders was consistently greater than that of the runners, swimmers, and controls.

A similar study supports these findings. Researchers in Finland compared the bone densities of women competing in four separate sports: orienteering (a form of hiking), cross-country skiing, cycling, and weight lifting. Overall, the weight lifters had higher bone mineral densities at most sites. The researchers commented that "weight training seems to provide more effective osteogenic [bone-forming] stimulus than endurance training."

A benefit of weight training is that it allows you to target specific bones for strengthening—just as you can target specific muscles for toning. Let's say a peripheral test reveals low bone density in your forearm. Simply choose weight-training exercises that work the forearm and challenge it accordingly. That way, weaker bones get extra attention.

With weight training, don't women build bulky muscles?

No! The reason men build bulk is because their bodies are naturally loaded with testosterone, a hormone that develops sex characteristics, including large muscles. Women have minute quantities of this hormone, but not enough to build man-sized muscles.

Women also have smaller muscle fibers than men do—another reason you won't build muscular bulk. What you will build, however, is stronger bones and muscle. Weight training is one of the best activities you can pursue for health and longevity.

How do I start a weight-training program?

To begin with, be sure you have no preexisting medical problems that could be aggravated by exercise. Have a physical and get your physician's approval before beginning any exercise program.

If you're new to weight training, your best bet is to work your entire body three days a week, on nonconsecutive days. This schedule gives your body time to rest so that it can respond by increasing bone and muscle strength. In addition, work with a qualified personal trainer who can show you the ropes.

Weight training routines are organized into *repetitions* (the number of times you lift a weight) and *sets* (a series of repetitions). A good weight-training routine for beginners consists of about three sets of ten exercises using dumbbells, barbells, or weight-training machines. Exercises should develop each major muscle group of the body, including shoulders, arms, chest, legs, upper and lower back, and abdomen. Areas of the body shown to be low in bone density, as identified by a bone density test, should be targeted. Ask your trainer which exercises are appropriate.

On the first set of each exercise, use a weight that feels relatively light to you and perform approximately 12 to 15 repetitions. Increase the poundage on the second set so that you can do about 10 to 12 repetitions. On the last set, up your poundage even more, using a weight that lets you lift about 6 to 8 repetitions. By progressively increasing your weights from workout to workout, you challenge your bones and muscles to strengthen.

Follow strict form as you exercise. Incorrect form reduces stress on the muscles and bones and can lead to injury. Here are some general guidelines for proper form:

- Be careful to move only the joints and body parts specified for each exercise.

- Take a firm grip on the bar so you will not accidentally drop the weights. On standing exercises, distribute your weight equally on each leg. This will keep you from losing balance and possibly injuring yourself. Also, bend your knees slightly to protect your lower back.

- To get the most from every repetition, lift the weight through a complete *range of motion*. Range of motion is the full path of an exercise, from extension to contraction and back again.

- Stress muscle groups with maximum intensity. Always strive to progressively increase your poundages. This is the only way to ensure optimal results.

- Perform the lifting and lowering motions in a slow, controlled fashion. That way, you'll better zero in on the muscles being worked. Fast, jerky repetitions, on the other hand, don't isolate muscles but instead place harmful stress on the joints, ligaments, and tendons. Not only is this an unproductive way to tone muscles, it's also a dangerous exercise habit to adopt because it increases your risk of injury.

- Breathe properly. With every repetition, inhale just before the lift and exhale as you complete it. Try to synchronize inhalation and exhalation rhythmically with the motion of the rep. Never hold your breath either. Holding your breath cuts oxygen supply to the blood and, coupled with the exertion of the lift, could cause light-headedness or fainting.

- Know your limits. Handling weights that are too heavy can lead to strains, a condition characterized by swelling and pain in muscles, and pulls, which are acute tears of muscle fibers. To avoid these injuries, increase your poundages gradually. Do not overdo.

How long will it take to get results?
Everyone will respond differently, depending on your diet and other lifestyle habits. But your bone density could increase in as little as three weeks, particularly if

you weight-train. That possibility is based on a study conducted with weight lifters. At the beginning of their training program, bone density in their forearms was the same as that of a control group, but increased significantly after three weeks.

The positive effects of exercise aren't permanent unless you keep it up. Researchers have found that if you stop working out, your bone density will return to where it was before you started your exercise program.

What about other forms of exercise?

Even though weight training appears to be the top bone-toning activity, other forms of exercise are effective too. Some of the best bone-building aerobic exercises appear to be walking, jogging, aerobic dance classes, and step aerobic classes—all considered to be weight-bearing exercise too.

A study of women 25 to 34 years old showed that a combination of regular exercise (running and walking) and ample calcium intake—either by diet or supplementation—can build bone mass in the lower spine by up to 15 percent.

So can dancing. A study of twenty-eight women (their average age was 67) demonstrated that dancing three times a week could significantly increase bone mineral density in the spine in those women already diagnosed with osteoporosis.

Other research with women shows that aerobic exercise does an admirable job of shoring up bone density in the hip region.

One form of exercise that doesn't receive high marks from bone researchers is swimming. Even though swimming tones up your cardiovascular system and is good for joints, the water buoys up your body and reduces stress on your bones. The result: less bone build-up.

You should perform aerobic exercise regularly during the week. Aerobic exercise enhances cardiovascular fitness, controls weight, and confers numerous other health benefits.

Probably, a combination of weight training and aerobics is the best thing you can do for your body and bones. A study conducted at the University of California discovered that a well-balanced exercise program—one that included weight training and aerobics—led to greater gains in bone density than either type alone. This particular study was conducted with men, however. Nonetheless, it hints at the benefits of diversifying your exercise program, no matter what your sex.

How often should I work out?

No one is 100 percent sure on what the optimum amount of exercise is per week to build and maintain bone health. But there is research that provides some clues. One study, for instance, found that you can build up bones throughout your body in as little as three hours a week of aerobics and weight training.

Some researchers believe you can get too much of a good thing—that overexercising could increase your vulnerability to bone trouble. In a study conducted at Stanford University, women who exercised for up to five hours a week increased bone strength in their spines. But women who worked out in excess of five hours a week had poor bone strength.

One type of weight-bearing exercise you can probably do most days of the week is walking. That's because it's relatively safe, easy to do, and convenient. In fact, research suggests that walking twenty to thirty minutes every day (or for one hour three times a week) is effective for building bone. Looking at it another way, one study demonstrated that women who walked more than 7.5 miles a week had greater bone density than those who walked less than a mile.

The bottom line is this: To get the bone-protective benefits of exercise, try to work out at least five times a week, with a mixture of aerobic and strength-developing exercise. Two to three times a week, engage in forty-five to sixty minutes of strength-developing exercise; at least three times a week, exercise aerobically for at least thirty minutes each session.

Glossary

AccuDEXA. A tabletop bone density test that uses dual-energy X-ray absorptiometry (DXA) to evaluate bone mineral density in the middle portion of the third finger.

Alendronate (Fosamax). A drug of the bisphosphonate class approved by the Food and Drug Administration (FDA) for the prevention and treatment of osteoporosis. Alendronate works by accumulating in the bone and making it more resistant to breakdown.

Bone densitometer. A machine that performs bone mineral density testing. It uses two X-ray beams that can detect the difference between bone and soft tissue.

Bone formation. The process by which bone cells (osteoblasts) synthesize the protein framework upon which crystals of calcium phosphate are deposited.

Bone markers. By-products of bone formation and bone resorption that are detectable in urine or blood. Measuring levels of bone markers, by urine or blood tests, is one method of monitoring the effectiveness of osteoporosis treatments or detecting bone disease.

Bone mass. The total amount of mineralized bone tissue within a specific bone or region.

Bone matrix. A latticelike structure of tough protein fibers upon which bone minerals are deposited.

Bone mineral content. The amount of bone mineral present at a specific site of a scan.

Bone mineral density. The amount of mineral in any given area or volume of bone. When the bone mineral content is divided by the area or volume assessed at a specific site, a value for bone density is provided.

Bone mineral density testing. A diagnostic test to determine the bone density in the spine, femur, forearm, wrist, or heel. Also called bone densitometry.

Bone resorption. The breakdown of bone by cells called osteoclasts. Osteoporosis occurs when bone resorption is greater than bone formation.

Calcidiol. An inactive form of vitamin D.

Calcitonin. A hormone secreted by the thyroid gland. Salmon calcitonin, a synthetic hormone, slows the rate of bone resorption by osteoclasts.

Calcitriol. The active form of vitamin D. Also, a synthetic form of vitamin D that aids calcium absorption and mineralization of bone. Calcitriol is a possible treatment for osteoporosis.

Calcium. The principal mineral constituent of bone.

Calcium phosphate. The mineralized structure of bone. Calcium phosphate is measured in bone density tests.

Central bone density measurements. Measurements of the spine or hip.

Collagen. A fibrous protein found in connective tissue,

including skin, bone, ligaments, and cartilage. About 30 percent of total body protein is composed of collagen.

Cortical bone. The hard outer layer of bone.

Dual-energy X-ray absorptiometry (DXA). The gold standard in bone density testing. It uses photons generated by an X-ray tube at two energy levels. DXA provides fast, accurate measurements of the hip, spine, and full body, with little radiation exposure.

Dual photon absorptiometry (DPA). A bone density measurement test that uses photons at two energy levels to measure the total cortical and trabecular mineral content of the hip, spine, and full body. A predecessor to DXA.

Estrogen. A female sex hormone produced mainly by the ovaries. Estrogen influences bone density by slowing the rate of bone resorption and improving the absorption of calcium.

Estrogen replacement therapy (ERT). Treatment that restores estrogen lost when natural estrogen production falls off due to menopause. Also called hormone replacement therapy (HRT).

Femur. The thighbone, which extends from the hip to the knee. It is the longest and strongest bone in the body.

Femoral head. A globe-shaped portion of the femur.

Femoral neck. A pyramid-shaped portion of the femur that is measured in bone density tests.

Femoral shaft. The long, uppermost portion of the thighbone.

Fracture. A break in a bone.

Glycoprotein. A protein in the bone matrix that helps reinforce bone.

Hormones. Chemicals that are secreted in body fluids and carried to organs to produce specific metabolic effects.

Hormone replacement therapy (HRT). A general term for all types of estrogen replacement therapy when given along with progestin.

Ipriflavone. A synthetic phytoestrogen that mimics the effect of estrogen in the body and confers numerous bone-protecting and bone-building benefits. Available in the United States as a nutritional supplement.

Isoflavones. A group of naturally occurring compounds in plants that exert effects similar to bodily estrogen.

Kyphosis. Curvature of the spine.

Magnetic resonance imaging (MRI). An emerging technology in the field of bone densitometry. MRI uses powerful magnetism, radio waves, and computer technology to produce detailed pictures of internal parts of the body.

Menopause. The time in a woman's life when her menstrual period ends. Levels of estrogen fall at this time because the ovaries cease their reproductive function.

Normal bone mass. Bone density within one standard deviation of the average for young normal adults (T-score above -1).

Osteoblast. A bone cell involved in forming new bone, repairing damaged bone, and replacing old bone.

Osteocalcin. The major noncollagen protein in bone.

Osteoclast. A bone cell that breaks down and removes old bone tissue.

Osteopenia. Low bone mass. A T-score between 1.0 and 2.5 standard deviations below the average (-1 and -2.5) indicates osteopenia.

p-DEXA. A tabletop scanner that uses dual-energy X-ray absorptiometry to evaluate bone density in the forearm.

Peak bone mass. The maximum bone density and strength accumulated during young adult life. Bone mass normally peaks at about age 30 in women.

Perimenopause. A period of fluctuating estrogen levels that hits about two years prior to menopause and continues for the next two years following menopause.

Peripheral bone measurements. Bone density measurements of outlying areas of the skeleton, such as fingers, forearm, wrist, or heel.

Peripheral Instantaneous X-ray Imager bone densitometer (PIXI). A small densitometer that uses dual-energy X-ray absorptiometry to measure bone density in the heel.

Photon. A unit of electromagnetic energy that is absorbed at a different rate by bone than by soft tissue.

Phytoestrogens. Compounds in plant foods that function as estrogens.

Postmenopause. A naturally occurring stage of life in which a woman has been free of menstrual periods for at least one year.

pQCT. A special-purpose version of quantitative computed tomography that evaluates bone density in the wrist and forearm.

Premenopause. The period prior to menopause.

Primary osteoporosis. Progressive bone loss that results from menopause or advancing age.

Proteoglycan. A protein in the bone matrix that helps reinforce bone.

Quantitative computed tomography (QCT). A diagnostic X-ray test used to measure trabecular bone density in the spine, where changes in bone density can be most rapid. QCT looks at the bone in three dimensions.

Radiographic absorptiometry (RA). An X-ray technique that uses computer technology to evaluate bone density in the fingers.

Radiologist. A physician who specializes in the use of radiation energy to diagnose and treat disease.

Raloxifene (Evista). A member of a class of compounds called selective estrogen receptor modulators (SERMs), which provide the benefits of estrogen, but without its side effects.

Receptor. A physiological signal device located on the membrane of a cell. Receptors recognize substances such as hormones, nutrients, or drugs and allow access to the cell.

Remodeling. The process of replacing old bone with new bone through the activity of osteoblasts and osteoclasts.

Resorption. The breakdown of bone through the activity of osteoclasts.

Secondary osteoporosis. Bone loss caused by the effects of a disease or medication.

Severe osteoporosis. Osteoporosis characterized by

bone density that is 2.5 standard deviations below the average for normal young adults (T-score at or below −2.5) and by the incidence of at least one fragility-related fracture. Also called established osteoporosis.

Single-energy X-ray absorptiometry (SXA). A diagnostic test that emits a single beam of radiation to assess bone density in the forearm or the heel.

Single photon absorptiometry (SPA). A diagnostic test that uses photons at a single energy level to measure bone mineral density in the wrist, forearm, and heel bone.

Sodium fluoride. An essential trace mineral that has been found to stimulate osteoblast activity and increase bone density.

Standard deviation. A measure of variation of distribution.

Trabecular bone. The interior portion of the bone. It is also known as spongy bone because it has a porous, spongelike structure. Trabecular bone, which provides extra strength for the cortical bone, may be preferentially lost in osteoporosis.

Trochanters. Two bony projections in the femur, called the greater trochanter and the lesser trochanter. The trochanters, which attach to muscles involved in hip movement, are frequently the site of osteoporotic fractures.

T-score. The number of standard deviations above or below the average bone mineral density for young normal adults.

Ultrasound densitometry. A diagnostic test used to measure bone density in the heel.

Vertebrae. The bones of the spine.

Vitamin D. Obtained mainly from sunlight and fortified dairy products, Vitamin D helps your body absorb calcium and break down phosphorus, a mineral required for bone formation.

Ward's triangle. A site located within the femoral neck that is very high in trabecular bone.

Z-score. The number of standard deviations above or below the average bone mineral density for individuals of the same age.

References

A portion of the information in this book comes from medical research reports in both popular and scientific publications, professional textbooks and booklets, promotional literature from supplement companies, case studies, Internet sources, and computer searches of medical databases of research abstracts.

INTRODUCTION:
THE TEST THAT CAN SAVE YOUR LIFE

Braun, W. 1997. Do your bones pass the test? *Saturday Evening Post,* 13 March, 18–20.

Burcum, J. 1999. Bone scan new weapon in fighting osteoporosis. *Minneapolis Star Tribune,* 4 August, 1E.

Genant, H. K., G. Guglielmi, and M. Jergas (eds.). 1998. *Bone densitometry and osteoporosis.* New York: Springer.

Health Technology Advisory Committee. 1998. Bone densitometry as a screening tool for osteoporosis in postmenopausal women. *Radiology Management* 20:43–54.

Jiang, C., M. L. Giger, and S. M. Kwak. 2000. Normalized bone mineral density as a predictor of bone strength. *Academic Radiology* 7:33–39.

Kulak, C. A. M., and J. P. Bilezikian. 1999. Bone mass measurement in identification of women at risk for osteoporosis. *International Journal of Fertility and Women's Medicine* 44:269–278.

Lenchik, L., P. Rochmis, and D. J. Sartoris. 1998. Optimized interpretation and reporting of dual X-ray absorptiometry (DXA) scans. *American Journal of Roentgenology* 171:1509–1520.

McCord, H. 1998. How are your bones? You—and your doctor—probably have no idea. *Prevention,* June, 106–114.

Meunier, P. J., P. D. Delmas, R. Eastell, et al. 1999. Diagnosis and management of osteoporosis in postmenopausal women: clinical guidelines. *Clinical Therapeutics* 21:1025–1044.

Miller, P. D., S. L. Bonnick, and C. Rosen. 1995. Guidelines for the clinical utilization of bone mass measurement in the adult population. *Calcified Tissue International* 57:251–252.

Padus, E., C. Perlmutter, and H. McCord. 1996. Size up your bones now. *Prevention,* February, 74.

Roan, S. 1995. No excuses: Women need to have bone testing. *Newsday,* 20 November, B13.

CHAPTER ONE: WHAT'S HAPPENING TO MY BONES?

Bisacre, M., et al. 1984. *The illustrated encyclopedia of the human body.* New York: Exeter Books.

Genant, H. K., G. Guglielmi, and M. Jergas (eds.). 1998 *Bone densitometry and osteoporosis.* New York: Springer.

Germano, C., and W. Cabot. 1999. *The osteoporosis solution.* New York: Kensington Books.

Gray, H. 1977. *Gray's anatomy.* New York: Crown Publishers.

Zuidema, G. D. 1986. *The John Hopkins atlas of human functional anatomy.* 3rd ed. Baltimore: John Hopkins University Press.

CHAPTER TWO: WILL I GET OSTEOPOROSIS?

Aloia, J. F., A. Vaswani, J. K. Yeh, et al. 1996. Risk for osteoporosis in black women. *Calcified Tissue International* 59:415–423.

Antonios, T. F., and G. A. MacGregor. 1995. Deleterious effects of salt intake other than effects on blood pressure. *Clinical and Experimental Pharmacology and Physiology* 22:180–184.

Brot, C., N. R. Jorgensen, and O. H. Sorensen. 1999. The influence of smoking on vitamin D status and calcium metabolism. *European Journal of Clinical Nutrition* 53: 920–926.

Calvo, M. S. 1994. The effects of high phosphorus intake on calcium homeostasis. *Advances in Nutritional Research* 9:183–207.

Editor. 1999. Higher blood pressure, weaker bones? *Health News* 5:7.

Felson, D. T., Y. Zhang, M. T. Hannan, et al. 1995. Alcohol intake and bone mineral density in elderly men and women. The Framington study. *American Journal of Epidemiology* 142:485–492.

Genant, H. K., G. Guglielmi, and M. Jergas. (eds.). 1998. *Bone densitometry and osteoporosis.* New York: Springer.

Gonzalez-Calvin, J. L., A. Garcia-Sanchez, V. Bellot, et al. 1993. Mineral metabolism, osteoblastic function and bone mass in chronic alcoholism. *Alcohol and Alcoholism* 28:571–579.

Hadjidakis, D., E. Kokkinakis, M. Sfakianakis, and S. A. Raptis. 1999. The type and time of menopause as decisive factors for bone mass changes. *European Journal of Clinical Investigation* 29:877–885.

Harris, S. S., and B. Dawson-Hughes. 1994. Caffeine and bone loss in healthy postmenopausal women. *American Journal of Clinical Nutrition* 60:573–578.

Iqbal, M. M. 2000. Osteoporosis: epidemiology, diagnosis, and treatment. *Southern Medical Journal* 93:2–18.

Kanis, J. A., P. Delmas, R. Burckhardt, et al. 1997. Guidelines for diagnosis and management of osteoporosis. *Osteoporosis International* 7:390–406.

Kazanjian, A., C. J. Green, K. Bassett, et al. 1999. Bone
    density testing in social context. *International Journal
    of Technology Assessment in Health Care* 15:679–685.

Lenchik, L., P. Rochmis, and D. J. Sartoris. 1998. Opti-
    mized interpretation and reporting of dual X-ray absorp-
    tiometry (DXA) scans. *American Journal of Roentgen-
    ology* 171:1509–1520.

Rico, H. 1990. Alcohol and bone disease. *Alcohol and Al-
    coholism* 25:345–352.

Swezey, R. L., and J. Adams. 1999. Fibromyalgia: a risk
    factor for osteoporosis. *Journal of Rheumatology* 26:
    2642–2644.

Takada, H., K. Washino, and H. Iwata. 1997. Risk factors
    for low bone mineral density among females: the effect
    of lean body mass. *Preventive Medicine* 26:633–638.

Treasure, J., and L. Serpell. 1999. Osteoporosis in anorexia
    nervosa. *Hospital Medicine* 60:477–480.

CHAPTER THREE:
HOW DO I KNOW IF MY BONE DENSITY IS LOW?

Delmas, P. D., and M. Fraser. 1999. Strong bones in later
    life: luxury or necessity? *Bulletin of the World Health
    Organization* 77:416–422.

Editor. 1997. Depression linked to fracture risk. *USA Today
    Magazine*. October 1997, vol. 126. no .2629.

Foundation for Osteoporosis Research and Education.
    1998. Guidelines of care on osteoporosis for the primary
    care physician. Online: www.fore.org/guide/exec.html.

Genant, H. K., G. Guglielmi, and M. Jergas. (eds.). 1998.
    Bone densitometry and osteoporosis. New York:
    Springer.

MacReady, N. 2000. Wrist fracture a red flag for osteo-
    porosis. Online: WebMD Medical News, www.webmd.
    com.

Malesky, G. 1986. Revitalize your spine. *Prevention*,
    March, 67–71.

Orr-Walker, B. J., M. C. Evans, R. W. Ames, et al. 1997.
    Premature hair graying and bone mineral density. *Jour-*

nal of Clinical Endocrinology and Metabolism 82:3580–3583.

Rosen, C. J., M. F. Holick, and P. S. Millard. 1994. Premature graying of hair is a risk marker for osteopenia. *Journal of Clinical Endocrinology and Metabolism* 79: 854–857.

CHAPTER FOUR: WHAT IS A DXA TEST?

Baran, D. T., K. G. Faulkner, H. K. Genant, et al. 1997. Diagnosis and management of osteoporosis: guidelines for the utilization of bone densitometry. *Calcified Tissue International* 61:433–440.

Donohue, P. 1998. Tests for bone density can detect sturdiness and find osteoporosis. *St. Louis Dispatch,* 4 February, 2E.

Genant, H. K., G. Guglielmi, and M. Jergas. (eds.). 1998. *Bone densitometry and osteoporosis.* New York: Springer.

Ferguson, T., and D. Sobel. 1998. Bone mineral density: test overview. Online: www.allHealth.com.

Kennedy, M. 1999. Boning up on osteoporosis. *WMJ: Official Publication of the State Medical Society of Wisconsin* 98:20–25.

Kleerekoper, M. 1998. Detecting osteoporosis. Beyond the history and physical examination. *Postgraduate Medicine* 103:45–47.

Kulak, C. A. M., and J. P. Bilezikian. 1999. Bone mass measurement in identification of women at risk for osteoporosis. *International Journal of Fertility and Women's Medicine* 44:269–278.

Lenchik, L., P. Rochmis, and D. J. Sartoris. 1998. Optimized interpretation and reporting of dual X-ray absorptiometry (DXA) scans. *American Journal of Roentgenology* 171:1509–1520.

McCord, H. 1998. How are your bones? You—and your doctor—probably have no idea. *Prevention,* 1 June, 106–114.

Miller, P. D., S. L. Bonnick, and C. Rosen. 1995. Guidelines for the clinical utilization of bone mass measurement in the adult population. *Calcified Tissue International* 57:251–252.

Nidus Information Services. 1998. What will confirm a diagnosis of osteoporosis? Online: www.well-connected. com.

Rossini, M., O. Viapiana, and S. Adami. 1998. Instrumental diagnosis of osteoporosis. *Aging* 10:240–248.

Strange, C. 1996. Boning up on osteoporosis. *FDA Consumer Magazine*. Online: www.fda.gov/fdac/features/ 796_bone.html.

Taxel, P. 1998. Osteoporosis: detection, prevention, and treatment in primary care. *Geriatrics* 53:22–29.

Truscott, J. G., J. Devlin, and P. Emery, 1996. DXA scanning. *Balliere Clinical Rheumatology* 10:679–698.

Woodhead, G. A., and M. M. Moss. 1998. Osteoporosis: diagnosis and prevention. *The Nurse Practitioner* 23:18, 23–27, 31–32.

CHAPTER FIVE: HOW DO I INTERPRET MY RESULTS?

Brody, J. E. 1998. Osteoporosis guidelines aim to prevent bone loss. *Minneapolis Star Tribune*, 18 November, 3E.

Kanis, J. A., P. Delmas, and P. Burckhardt. 1997. Guidelines for diagnosis and management of osteoporosis. *Osteoporosis International* 7:390–406.

Lenchik, L., P. Rochmis, and D. J. Sartoris. 1998. Optimized interpretation and reporting of dual X-ray absorptiometry (DXA) scans. *American Journal of Roentgenology* 171:1509–1520.

Lunar. 2000. DEXA results explained. (Information guide for physicians and institutions.)

Strange, C. 1999. The bare bones of osteoporosis. 5 October. Online: www.onhealth.com.

Taxel, P. 1998. Osteoporosis: detection, prevention, and treatment in primary care. *Geriatrics* 53:22–29.

Woodhead, G. A., and M. M. Moss. 1998. Osteoporosis: diagnosis and prevention. *The Nurse Practitioner* 23:18, 23–27, 31–32.

CHAPTER SIX: ARE THERE OTHER TESTS?

Arnaud, C. 1996. Osteoporosis: using "bone markers" for diagnosis and monitoring. *Geriatrics* 51:24–27.

Augat, P., T. Fuerst, and H. K. Genant. 1998. Quantitative bone mineral assessment at the forearm: a review. *Osteoporosis International* 8:299–310.

Baran, D. T., K. G. Faulkner, H. K. Genant, et al. 1997. Diagnosis and management of osteoporosis: guidelines for the utilization of bone densitometry. *Calcified Tissue International* 61:433–440.

Braun, W. 1997. Do your bones pass the test? *Saturday Evening Post,* 13 March, 18–20.

Burcum, J. 1999. Bone scan new weapon in fighting osteoporosis. *Minneapolis Star Tribune,* 4 August, 1E.

Editor. 1998. Bone ultrasonometry: Achilles+ receives U.S. market approval. *Lunar Osteoporosis Update,* July, 1.

Ferguson, T., and D. Sobel. 1998. Bone mineral density: test overview. Online: www.allHealth.com.

Fischer, M., and F. Raue. 1999. Measurements of bone mineral density. Mineral density in metabolic bone disease. *The Quarterly Journal of Nuclear Medicine* 43: 233–240.

Genant, H. K., G. Guglielmi, and M. Jergas. (eds.). 1998. *Bone densitometry and osteoporosis.* New York: Springer.

Grampp, S., M. Jergas, C. C. Gluer, et al. 1993. Radiologic diagnosis of osteoporosis. Current methods and perspectives. *Radiologic Clinics of North America* 31:1133–1145.

Kennedy, M. 1999. Boning up on osteoporosis. *WMJ: Official Publication of the State Medical Society of Wisconsin* 98: 20–25.

Kleerekoper, M. 1997. Which bone density measurement? *Journal of Bone and Mineral Research* 12:712–714.

Kleerekoper, M. 1998. Detecting osteoporosis. Beyond the history and physical examination. *Postgraduate Medicine* 103:45–47.

Lenchik, L., P. Rochmis, and D. J. Sartoris. 1998. Optimized interpretation and reporting of dual X-ray absorptiometry (DXA) scans. *American Journal of Roentgen-ology* 171:1509–1520.

Limpaphayom, K., S. Bunyavejchevin, and N. Taechakrai-chana. 1998. Similarity of bone mass measurement among hip, spines and distal forearm. *Journal of the Medical Association of Thailand* 81:94–97.

Ross, P. D. 1997. Radiographic absorptiometry for measur-ing bone mass. *Osteoporosis International* 7:S103–S107.

Rossini, M., O. Viapiana, and S. Adami. 1998. Instrumental diagnosis of osteoporosis. *Aging* 10:240–248.

Taxel, P. 1998. Osteoporosis: detection, prevention, and treatment in primary care. *Geriatrics* 53:22–29.

Woodhead, G. A., and M. M. Moss. 1998. Osteoporosis: diagnosis and prevention. *The Nurse Practitioner* 23:18, 23–27, 31–32.

CHAPTER SEVEN:
BASED ON MY RESULTS, WHAT'S NEXT?

Foundation for Osteoporosis Research and Education. 1998. Guidelines of care on osteoporosis for the primary care physician. Online: www.fore.org/guide/exec.html.

Genant, H. K., G. Guglielmi, and M. Jergas. (eds.). 1998. *Bone densitometry and osteoporosis.* New York: Springer.

Iqbal, M. M. 2000. Osteoporosis: epidemiology, diagnosis, and treatment. *Southern Medical Journal* 93:2–18.

Meunier, P. J., P. D. Delmas, R. Eastell, et al. 1999. Di-agnosis and management of osteoporosis in postmeno-pausal women: clinical guidelines. *Clinical Therapeutics* 21:1025–1044.

Padus, E. 1996. Size up your bones now. *Prevention,* Feb-ruary, 74–81, 130–138.

CHAPTER EIGHT:
WHICH NUTRIENTS BUILD BONE DENSITY?

Allen, L. H. 1982. Calcium bioavailability and absorption: a review. *The American Journal of Clinical Nutrition,* April, 35.

American Dental Association. 1999. Questions and answers on fluoride. Online: www.ada.org.

American Dietetic Association. 1994. Position of the American Dietetic Association: the impact of fluoride on dental health. *Journal of the American Dietetic Association* 94:1428.

Brown, J. 1990. *The science of human nutrition*. San Diego: Harcourt Brace Jovanovich.

Editor. 1984. Consensus conference: osteoporosis. *Journal of the American Medical Association* 252:799–802.

Editor. 1999. Can taking magnesium supplements help keep my bones strong? *Mayo Clinic Health Letter* 17:8.

Eisinger, J., and D. Clairnet. 1993. Effects of silicon, fluoride, etidronate and magnesium on bone mineral density: a retrospective study. *Magnesium Research* 6:247–249.

Freeland-Graves, J. H. 1988. Manganese: an essential nutrient for humans. *Nutrition Today,* November/December, 13–19.

Griffith, H. W. 1988. *Complete guide to vitamins, minerals and supplements*. Tucson, Arizona: Fisher Books.

Kirschmann, J. D. 1979. *Nutrition almanac*. New York: McGraw-Hill.

Kleerekoper, M. 1998. The role of fluoride in the prevention of osteoporosis. *Endocrinology and Metabolism Clinics of North America* 27:441–452.

Leveille, S. G., A. Z. LaCroix, T. D. Koepsell, et al. 1997. Dietary vitamin C and bone mineral density in postmenopausal women in Washington state, USA. *Journal of Epidemiology and Community Health* 51:479–485.

Liebman, B. 1992. Nutrition and aging. *Nutrition Action Healthletter* 19:1–4.

Newnham, R. E. 1994. Essentiality of boron for healthy bones and joints. *Environmental Health Perspectives* 102:83–85.

Nidus Information Services. 1998. Osteoporosis. Online: www.well-connected.com.

Nielson, F. H. 1988. Boron—an overlooked element of potential nutritional importance. *Nutrition Today,* January/February, 4–7.

Pacelli, L. C. 1989. To fortify bones use calcium and exercise. *The Physician and Sportsmedicine* 7:27–28.

Power, M. L., R. P. Heaney, and H. J. Kalkwarf. 1999. The role of calcium in health and disease. *American Journal of Obstetrics and Gynecology* 181:1560–1569.

Saltman, P. D., and L. G. Strause. 1993. The role of trace minerals in osteoporosis. *Journal of the American College of Nutrition* 12:384–389.

Sizer, F., and E. Whitney. 1997. *Nutrition concepts and controversies.* 7th ed. Belmont, Calif.: West/Wadsworth.

Sojka, J. E., and C. M. Weaver. 1995. Magnesium supplementation and osteoporosis. *Nutrition Review* 53:71–74.

Stenson, J. 1995. Fluoride-calcium boosts bone mass. *Medical Tribune for the Family Physician.* 12 October, 1, 8.

Strause, L., P. Saltman, K. T. Smith, et al. 1994. Spinal bone loss in postmenopausal women supplemented with calcium and trace minerals. *Journal of Nutrition* 124: 1060–1064.

Tranquilli, A. L., E. Lucino, G. G. Garzetti, et al. 1994. Calcium, phosphorus and magnesium intakes correlate with bone mineral content in postmenopausal women. *Gynecological Endocrinology* 8:55–58.

Vaughn, L. 1984. Calcium: the white healer. *Prevention,* November, 79–80, 95–96.

Volpe, S. L., L. J. Taper, and S. Meacham. 1993. The relationship between boron and magnesium status and bone mineral density in the human: a review. *Magnesium Research* 6:291–296.

Weber, P. 1999. The role of vitamins in the prevention of osteoporosis—a brief status report. *International Journal for Vitamin and Nutrition Research* 69:194–197.

CHAPTER NINE:
HOW CAN I PLAN A BONE-HEALTHY DIET?

Barth, C. A., and U. Behnke. 1997. Nutritional physiology of whey and whey components. *Nahrung* 41:2–12.

Bonjour, J. P., M. A. Schurch, and R. Rizzoli. 1996. Nutritional aspects of hip fractures. *Bone* 18:139S–144S.

Bounous, G., G. Batist, and P. Gold. 1991. Whey proteins in cancer prevention. *Cancer Letter* 57:91–94.

Cassidy, A., S. Bingham, and K. D. R. Setchell. 1994. Biological effects of a diet of soy protein rich in isoflavones on the menstrual cycle of premenopausal women. *American Journal of Clinical Nutrition* 60:333–340.

Chiechi, L. M. 1999. Dietary phytoestrogens in the prevention of long-term postmenopausal diseases. *International Journal of Gynecology and Obstetrics* 67:39–40.

Davis, J. 2000. There's something to be said for having "tea bones." Online: WebMD Medical News, www.webmd.com.

Dwyer, J. T., B. R. Goldin, N. Sual, et al. 1994. Tofu and soy drinks contain phytoestrogens. *Journal of the American Dietetic Association* 94:739–743.

Editor. 1999. Fruits and veggies: bone boosters. *Health News* 5:5.

Feskanich, D., W. C. Willett, M. J. Stampfer, et al. 1996. Protein consumption and bone fractures in women. *American Journal of Epidemiology* 143:472–479.

Griffith, D. 1999. Bones and beyond. *Nutraceuticals World* 2:32–36.

Hegarty, V. M., H. M. May, and K. T. Khaw. 2000. Tea drinking and bone mineral density in older women. *American Journal of Clinical Nutrition* 71:1003–1007.

Keller, C., J. Fullerton, and C. Mobley. 1999. Supplemental and complementary alternatives to hormone replacement therapy. *Journal of the American Academy of Nurse Practitioners* 11:187–198.

Kerstetter, J. E., K. O. O'Brien, and K. L. Insogna. 1998. *American Journal of Clinical Nutrition* 68:859–865.

Lau, E. M., T. Kwok, J. Hoo, et al. 1998. Bone mineral density in Chinese elderly female vegetarians, vegans, lacto-vegetarians and omnivores. *European Journal of Clinical Nutrition* 52:60–64.

Messina, M. J. 1994. Dietary phytoestrogens: cancer cause or prevention. *The Soy Connection* 3:1–4.

Munger, R. G., J. R. Cerhan, and B. C. Chiu. 1999. Prospective study of dietary protein intake and risk of hip fracture in postmenopausal women. *American Journal of Clinical Nutrition* 69:147–152.

Ohta, A., M. Ohtsuki, A. Hosona, et al. 1998. Dietary fructooligosaccharides prevent osteopenia after gastrecotomy in rats. *Journal of Nutrition* 128:106–110.

Power, M. L., R. P. Heaney, and H. J. Kalkwarf. 1999. The role of calcium in health and disease. *American Journal of Obstetrics and Gynecology* 181:1560–1569.

Takada, Y., S. Aoe, and M. Kumegawa. 1996. Whey protein stimulated the proliferation and differentiation of osteoblastic MC3T3-E1 cells. *Biochemical and Biophysical Research Communications* 223:445–449.

Tucker, K. L., M. T. Hannan, H. Chen, et al. 1999. Potassium, magnesium, and fruit and vegetable intakes are associated with greater bone mineral density in elderly men and women. *American Journal of Clinical Nutrition* 69:727–736.

Wohl, G. R., L. Loehrke, B. A. Watckins, et al. 1998. Effects of high-fat diet on mature bone mineral content, structure, and mechanical properties. *Calcified Tissue International* 63:74–79.

Zava, D. T. 1994. The phytoestrogen paradox. *The Soy Connection* 3:1–4.

CHAPTER TEN: WHAT MEDICINES ARE AVAILABLE TO TREAT OSTEOPOROSIS?

Head, K. A. 1999. Ipriflavone: an important bone-building isoflavone. *Alternative Medicine Review* 4:10–22.

Iqbal, M. M. 2000. Osteoporosis: epidemiology, diagnosis, and treatment. *Southern Medical Journal* 93:2–18.

Kanis, J. A., P. Delmas, R. Burckhardt, et al. 1997. Guidelines for diagnosis and management of osteoporosis. *Osteoporosis International* 7:390–406.

Kennedy, M. 1999. Boning up on osteoporosis. *WMJ: Official Publication of the State Medical Society of Wisconsin* 98:20–25.

Medical Economics Company. 1999. *Physicians' desk reference.* Montvale, N.J.: Medical Economics Company.

National Osteoporosis Foundation. 1999. *Physician's guide*

to prevention and treatment of osteoporosis. Washington, D.C.: National Osteoporosis Foundation.

Reginster, J. V., Y. Henrotin, and C. Gosset. 1999. Promising new agents in osteoporosis. *Drugs in R & D.* 1: 195–201.

Scheiber, M. D., and R. W. Rebar. 1999. Isoflavones and postmenopausal bone health: a viable alternative to estrogen therapy? *Menopause* 6:233–241.

CHAPTER ELEVEN: WHAT KIND OF EXERCISE
PROMOTES BONE DENSITY?

Bartels, R. L. 1992. Weight training: how to lift and eat for strength and power. *The Physician and Sportsmedicine* 20:233–234.

Branca, F. 1999. Physical activity, diet and skeletal health. *Public Health Nutrition* 2:391–396.

Danielson, D. L. 1981. Strengthen your bones with exercise. *Prevention,* July, 108–115.

Editor. 1987. Well-rounded exercise may build more bone. *Prevention,* August, 12.

Fiatarone, M. A., E. C. Marks, N. D. Ryan, et al. 1990. High-intensity strength training in nonagenarians: effect on skeletal muscle. *Journal of the American Medical Association* 263:3029–3034.

Halle, J. S., G. L. Smidt, K. D. O'Dwyer, et al. 1990. Relationship between trunk muscle torque and bone mineral content of the lumbar spine and hip in healthy postmenopausal women. *Physical Therapy* 70:690–700.

Heinonen, A., O. P. Kannus, and H. Sievanen. 1993. Bone mineral density of female athletes in different sports. *Bone and Mineral* 23:1–14.

Kelley, G. A. 1998. Aerobic exercise and bone density at the hip in postmenopausal women: a meta-analysis. *Preventive Medicine* 27:798–807.

Kudlacek, S., F. Pietschmann, P. Bernecker, et al. 1997. The impact of a senior dancing program on spinal and peripheral bone mass. *American Journal of Physical Medicine and Rehabilitation* 76:477–481.

Meiner, S. E. 1999. An expanding landscape. Osteoporosis.

Treatment options today. *Advance for Nurse Practitioners* 7:26–31, 80.

Nishimura, K. 1990. Moderate exercise may help prevent osteoporosis and prolong life. *Mature Health,* April, 8–9.

Nutter, J. 1986. Physical activity increases bone density. *National Strength and Conditioning Association Journal* 8:67–69.

Pacelli, L. C. 1989. To fortify bones use calcium and exercise. *The Physician and Sportsmedicine* 7:27–28.

Rogers, M. A., and W. J. Evans. 1993. Changes in skeletal muscle with aging: effects of exercise training. In: Holloszy, J. O. (ed.). *Exercise in Sports Sciences Review* 21: 65–66.

Schwade, S., and M. Stanten. 1996. Tone your bones. *Prevention*, November, 74–84.

Stamford, B. 1984. Weight-training principles. *The Physician and Sportsmedicine* 12:195.

Taylor, F. 1991. Building bones with bodybuilding. *The Physician and Sportsmedicine* March 19:51.

Ulrich, C. M., C. C. Georgiou, D. E. Gillis, et al. 1999. Lifetime physical activity is associated with bone mineral density in premenopausal women. *Journal of Women's Health* 8:365–375.

Welsh, L., and O. M. Rutherford. 1996. Hip bone density is improved by high-impact aerobic exercise in postmenopausal women and men over 50 years. *European Journal of Applied Physiology* 74:511–517.

Index

About the Author

Maggie Greenwood-Robinson, Ph.D., is one of the country's top health and medical authors. She is the author of *Hair Savers for Women: A Complete Guide to Preventing and Treating Hair Loss*; *The Cellulite Breakthrough*; *Natural Weight Loss Miracles*; *Kava: The Ultimate Guide to Nature's Anti-Stress Herb*; and *21 Days to Better Fitness*. Plus, she is the coauthor of nine other fitness books, including the national bestseller *Lean Bodies*; *Lean Bodies Total Fitness*; *High Performance Nutrition*; *Power Eating*; and *50 Workout Secrets*.

Her articles have appeared in *Let's Live*, *Physical*, *Great Life*, *Shape* magazine, *Christian Single* magazine, *Women's Sports and Fitness*, *Working Woman*, *Muscle and Fitness*, *Female Bodybuilding and Fitness*, and many other publications. She is a member of the Advisory Board of *Physical* magazine. In addition, she has a doctorate in nutritional counseling and is a certified nutritional consultant.